Vancouver Fiction

Edited
and with an Introduction by

DAVID WATMOUGH

POLESTAR PRESS
WINLAW BC

VANCOUVER FICTION

ISBN 0-919591-05-1

Published by

Polestar Press RR 1 Winlaw BC V0G 2J0 604 226 7670

Acknowledgements

Excerpt from the novel *The New Front Line*, reprinted by permission of Hubert Evans; *Down at English Bay* from the novel The Innocent Traveller by Ethel Wilson, reprinted by permission of the U.B.C. Library; *The Bravest Boat* by Malcolm Lowry copyright © 1961 by Margerie Bonner Lowry, and reprinted by permission of Literistic, Ltd.; *Ebbe & Hattie* from the collection Flycatcher, reprinted by permission of George Bowering; excerpt from the novel *Crossings* by Betty Lambert, reprinted by permission of the estate of Betty Lambert; excerpt from *Motet* by Keith Maillard, reprinted by permission of Stoddart Publishing, Toronto, Canada; *Heroes* printed by permission of Robert Harlow; *Laura*, an excerpt from Da Vinci's Light, printed by permission of Beverley Simons; *Recessional* by DM Fraser copyright © the estate of DM Fraser; *Trash* by permission of Audrey Thomas; *There are More Dark Women in the World Than Light* by permission of Keath Fraser; *Blessed are the Dead* by permission of Jane Rule; *Vancouver Summer Pudding* and the *Introduction* to Vancouver Fiction by permission of David Watmough.

Photo Credits

Hubert Evans photo courtesy Elizabeth Bakewell; Ethel Wilson photo courtesy Ethel Wilson Papers, U.B.C.; Malcolm Lowry photo courtesy Malcolm Lowry Papers, U.B.C.; George Bowering photo by Thea Bowering; Betty Lambert photo by Glen E. Erikson; Keith Maillard photo by Rhoda Williamson; Robert Harlow photo by Chuck Burns; Beverley Simons photo courtesy Beverley Simons; DM Fraser photo by Steve Nemeth; Audrey Thomas photo by Sam Tata; Keath Fraser photo courtesy Keath Fraser; Jane Rule photo by Dave Morgan; David Watmough photo by Edmund J O'Brien Photography.

Vancouver Fiction was designed by Julian Ross, with cover and initial capital lettering by Lou Lynn. It was produced by Polestar Press in Winlaw, BC and printed by Friesen Printers in Altona, Manitoba. September 1985.

Special thanks to Jack Shadbolt for permission to use his *Summer Suite* (panel 1) for our cover illustration.

VANCOUVER FICTION

CONTENTS

Introduction

The success of a story collection or an anthology such as this centennial celebration is largely contingent on a felicity of balance — so that the reader neither suffocates in a sea of harrowing tragedy nor is hanged on a rope of unmitigated merriment. With one's own work the task of establishing a correct equilibrium in a volume is solely determined by whatever one decides to include or exclude. But in this kind of assorted anthology it is not possible, nor is it at all desirable, to ask an author for a particular *kind* of story in the context of it being either upbeat or downbeat.

I certainly had no idea what these writers were going to come up with once they had accepted my invitation nor did I know what was going to emerge in terms of mood or how things would sit in juxtaposition. But what has emerged, I submit, is nothing less than extraordinary. I was frankly astonished at the patterns that began to take shape right from the start and which eventually coalesced into a distinct literary portrait of the city and its past which I do not think we have seen recorded elsewhere.

Time magazine described the Vancouver of the 1970s as the Rio de Janeiro of the northern hemisphere and, leaving that journal's hyperbole aside, the sheer beauty of place is a fact to be reckoned with by those living in Vancouver's orbit. What I think the unbiased reader will find here, though, is an honest witness to place and at the same time, a frequently dry, occasionally laconic, and generally detached sense of ease, which allows these writers a great faculty of range.

At the same broad level I must make mention of the unanticipated humour that flits about these narratives. It is rarely of the belly-laugh variety, although solid guffaw material is certainly there in George Bowering's volatile story. But more often the spectrum runs between the caustic to a Tio Peppe dryness. However, like the sunshine in these parts, this is an intermittent quality. Also, the cause for smiles, even wry ones, is usually counterpointed by the presence of clouds — silver-edged or not.

A travel writer, even a good one, could extract little useful data from these westcoast rooted fictions, for topographical and geographical data are utilized here as starting points rather than destinations. True, the mountains frequently serve as a metaphor but, considering their ubiquity, in a remarkably offhand way. I could not discern a single page owning to a sense of the city being *dragged* in as an unruly constituent — born either of obligation or a desire to pad the narrative. Yet the writing is soaked in its metropolitan incarnation to a degree which suggests it could derive the stuff of its existence from nowhere else. My explanation for this is that these authors are all, in some sense, geographers of the *mind* and thus the invocation of place names, the presence of the sea, mountains, westering sunlight and the insistence of rain remain only backdrops which can shape talk and modify action, but never *usurp* the human experience.

A few details relating to the generality of my contributors. . . . Only one is a native Vancouverite; Keath Fraser, the youngest in reputation. Interestingly enough, his story ranges furthest from his birthplace and perhaps itself suggests an augury for the future city. Only two of those here were born in the United Kingdom — Malcolm Lowry and myself, which might come as a surprise to those who feel the English overlay on Vancouver remains excessive or at least substantial. The United States has given us three authors presented here: Audrey Thomas, Keith Maillard and Jane Rule. South Africa was the birthplace of Ethel Wilson while the interior of the province has provided Robert Harlow from Prince Rupert and George Bowering from the Okanagan Valley. The rest of

Canada is represented by an Albertan, Betty Lambert; a Manitoban, Beverley Simons; one Ontarian, Hubert Evans; and from the Maritimes, D. M. Fraser. So there are seven native Canadians in all which is, hearteningly, more than half of the total.

There are, of course, many other Canadian and foreign authors who have lived in this city and its environs and written of such. At some time or other such eastern and prairie authors as Alice Munro, Margaret Laurence and Matt Cohen, to name just a trio, have lived in Vancouver and written memorably about the experience. But in the strict context of this book I decided that they are not "family" in the sense that the thirteen represented are.

The oldest of our authors was born when Vancouver was two-years old with the youngest arriving well into the second half of our city's existence. All have spent a substantial portion of their lives here and only one never became a Canadian citizen. I don't think it too fanciful to suggest that this international mix echoes the city's current complexion. But in saying that I am sorely conscious of the classic exception of those major ethnic constituents from Asia who are not represented by this cluster of authors, people who have already resoundingly shaped our local food habits, our architecture, our visual arts, and such visibly noticeable factors as our politics, our educational structures and our Pacific Rim awareness. My hope as a writer and citizen of this no mean city is that writers from the Asian sensibility would prevail in this book's historical successor in 2086.

To return to those presented here. What is as equally intriguing as the cultural mix of a group of writers with national and international reputations, drawn from a metropolitan population of less than a million and a half people, is their implicit significance. For literary communities, as with anthologies, exist on the iceberg principle. So that behind these thirteen stand a much greater phalanx of writers, including those with comparable reputation and talent but working in such areas as poetry, non-fiction, children's literature and playwriting. (The poets, at least, will be honored in this centennial context under the Polestar aegis with a companion volume to this.)

Finally, a few editorial comments on each of the baker's dozen stories offered, via the chronology of an evolving city rather than one suggesting either the dates when they were actually written or the birthdates of their creators.

We begin with an extract from Hubert Evans' 1927 novel, The New Front Line, where we find the promise of a young city allied to the promise of a westcoast spring. But from the outset there is underlying tension. The shadows from World War One — where the first 'Front Line' was seared in the memories of soldiers — thrust coldly forward into the urban future. There is a conflict, too, between the pull of the city and the attractions of an unspoiled wilderness. Then this latter theme is a thread running through the work of Hubert Evans who built his home on the Sunshine Coast in 1926 but who always maintained links wih the city a few miles across the water. Evans' Vancouver as he presents it here, is certainly intinct with postwar promise, but it is equally no Walt Disney creation. The balance between light and dark is struck: it will remain to the last page.

Ethel Wilson's *Down At English Bay* from The Innocent Traveller is a brilliant evocation of a between-wars Vancouver centering on Joe Fortes, the famed Black lifeguard and character of the West End's English Bay. My perception here is that the author's predominantly English literary sensibility is gently nudged aside as a colonial past is laid to rest and a unique city unfurling, with no easy terms of reference to anywhere else, begins to come into its own. There was plenty of gentility about the Vancouver world Ethel Wilson evokes here but in her cultivated yet steely vision, it never predominates.

To the purist, perhaps, Malcolm Lowry should not be here at all. I can recall a quarter of a century ago growing restless myself at the local Lowry industry as a boost for Canadian literature. After all, he never became a Canadian, came to British Columbia in maturity, leaving likewise to eventually die in his native land. But things have changed. I think we can now be more relaxed in our distinctions over famous visitors who have stayed at length and expatriate native sons. The city is now big enough, old enough, to take such matters in its stride.

In the segment *The Bravest Boat* from Hear Us O Lord From Heaven Thy Dwelling Place the Lost Lagoon in Stanley Park which Lowry describes houses that fountain which was erected to mark the fiftieth anniversary of the city. I have no evidence to show that the author was aware of the fact. No matter. We can let his contribution celebrate the halfway mark of our centenary and at the same time enjoy his evocation of a mythical Vancouver, named Enochvilleport, with its quite unmythical naming of the specific flora and fauna which few of his unBritish successors have been able or willing to do. For this English transplant, no lazy allusions to mere bushes and birds but to red cedar and buffleheads, mergansers and scaups. We get not just 'trees' but apples and hawthorns and weeping willows. And can quicken to the still pertinent accuracy of green dragons along the far side of Lost Lagoon "giving off their peculiar animal-like odour." We can equally appreciate that median stage when this evolving city with trees (was) making way "for grinning regiments of villas." And note that those stucco houses of the West End themselves dissolved to be superseded by the soaring fingers of the high-rises.

It is still Stanley Park but in a radically other mood, where we encounter glimpses and flashes of dreams in George Bowering's story *Ebbe & Hattie*, insouciant images first liberated in 1974. His Vancouver is truly the sum of its parts: the Kerrisdale (which was to flourish again much later in Bowering's verse), the quiet of the Endowment Lands and the great, romantic park at the mouth of the city with its prosaically numbered beaches. There is the dance of mutinous 'us' and stoopid 'them' tying dormitory, forest and recreation area into a multi-coloured backdrop for some irrepressible nose-thumbing. Then I find to my taste the irony of this Governor-General's Award-winner being the sole reminder in this selection that Vancouver was the counter-culture capital of Canada, with 4th Avenue in Kitsilano its 'Haight Ashbury'.

The lips may bend but in grimace, not smile, with our excerpt from the late Betty Lambert's brilliant Crossings, for the mood is sombre, the design dark in this rude and savage salvage of female living along the underbelly of Vancouver. This is not comfortable writing. It is the hostile antidote to media hype and the glossy clichés of our million and one calendars. But as our rain cleans so can our truth cleanse in the hands of a Lambert in a narrative where candour counts first and last. Crossings doesn't need defense or excuse but it is here, on the nerve-ends of existence, that we of all the genders, witness to a courageous woman's cathartic powers.

When we come to Keith Maillard's new novel, Motet, from which we present an extract, the mood may be somewhat surrealistic but the place is still Vancouver — with a pervasive sense of water falling as a central ingredient of local living. The rain and green of the vibrant vegetation are neither ever far away for the reader of these pages. Indeed, while the use of natural phenomena as a determing factor in conduct and even thought patterns are perceivable in several of these fictions, it is nowhere more the case than in Maillard's pages. And surely there is something especially germane to this place and its inhabitants when in his conclusion of this excerpt Vancouver is evoked as both home and as sanctuary behind the sheltering shoulders of the Rockies.

Heroes by Robert Harlow is a story with themes which comprise familiar landmarks for those conversant with his fictional territory. Then his is a westcoast signature which was established as long ago as 1962 with his novel Royal Murdoch and has never faltered through books like Scann and Paul Nolan, even though he has worked with a diversity of subjects from race-courses to the male menopause. Harlow is a writer who has found in this place somewhere he can work consistently, honing his craft, striving to deepen the imaginative reach, while not succumbing to each passing flicker of fictional fashion or stylistic bandwagon. With this author who was raised in Prince George before seeing the world, the geographic distance from there to the place he has lived for the majority of days since World War Two has not been very far. But we are dealing with a metropolitan area which is infinitely more a state of mind than an accuracy of longitude and latitude. Besides, Robert Harlow has always displayed a lively interest in *generational* distances. You know you are in Harlow-land when you come across such lines as: "There's seventeen years between us," he said.

With the excerpt *Laura* from the novel-in-progress by Vancouver's Beverley Simons we are introduced to the singular suburb nestled below the North Shore mountains known familiarly as 'West Van'. Simons proves again here in her fiction what she has so resoundingly demonstrated in her dramas, that she is an exemplar in the highlighting of the stresses and tensions common to the affluent societies of Western Europe and North America. Here in memorable precision she depicts the costly breakdown of familial units, the preoccupation with psychiatric problems, experimentation with life-styles (a sort of Marin County in microcosm) and real estate as some kind of uncertain panacea. In other words, a variegated panoply of human foible and aspiration against a splendidly impervious landscape. If, as we have said, Vancouver is a state of mind, Beverley Simon's West Van is that state of mind in crisis.

With *Recessional*, an original short story by the late D. M. Fraser, we are satisfyingly regaled with more dry wit from the wetlands — only here reinforced with a resonant chord of satire which is early struck and easily sustained throughout this terse tale. This transplanted Maritimer who made urban nightscape his peculiar realm offers us Fantasy City whose edges are blurred and mysteriously dim in its nocturnal pulse. The surrealism that dances, elflike, is rooted in a Vancouver context and our citizenry is intriguingly and deliciously conceived of as a species which worships beauty. And surely we can all embarrassedly vouchsafe that we have been dutiful parrots of that. . . .

From night into day, from downtown to residential district (but *never* outer-suburb) takes us from Fraser to Audrey Thomas, the bard of intimate domestic detail, local themes and connotations. "During July and August relatives visited, or friends . . ." evokes a familiar pattern for many of us adopted citizens. And the statement: "Vancouver was lovely in the sunshine, still is", is another comment that local readers will smile at for its unerring accuracy of flavour with just the right touch of defiance to what is ostensibly a commonplace. Then *Trash* has many a local nerve-end under writerly scrutiny. We perceive the palpable presence of Point Grey — or at least the vast university sprawled across its western extremity — as it informs both culturally and economically such contiguous communities as Dunbar and Kitsilano. And we are also delivered with disconcerting casualness that odd but accurate sense of Vancouver as a place where "everything is not quite what it seems." In the disarming language of the everyday and the benign aura that a beautiful location affords, Audrey Thomas demonstrates here in "Trash" that temples flush and hands tremble behind doors and above our ceilings. Yes indeed, says Thomas, this paradise is hyphenated with an inferno. Her palette contains the right colouring for both.

The title of Keath Fraser's story, *There Are More Dark Women in the World Than Light* is somewhat lengthier than the pointilliste dabs of evocation he employs to mount his portrait of contempory Vancouver. Then the nervous energy which animates this account of the Younger Set owns to a special restlessness which is perhaps *sui generis* in terms of the town and its time. The urban image here is a kind of climatic version of topographically restricted Hong Kong, while the same dry, laconic tone of present-day Vancouver evoked by

some of his fellow contributors is certainly here too. There are lots of caressing little local details from this native: Doug & The Slugs, the Whitecaps, the Dome, and the usually unheralded cherry-blossom time when Vancouver outmatches both Washington, D.C. and Tokyo. Yet sights and sounds are cellophaned in a cold chic which suggests, fascinatingly enough, a city non-existent and largely undreamed of even fifteen years ago. With Expo upon us perhaps all of Vancouver life prior to it is going to look quaint and miniscule before the decade has run its course. In which case even a Fraser up-to-the-minute comminiqué will become an archive.

Jane Rule's story *Blessed Are The Dead* proves to be a superb scouring of the picture-postcard image of our celestial city. It might also be described as a quicklime cocktail. It tackles sloppy sentiment with gusto and skilfully utilises that final counterpoint to meretricious hope — death. In a sense this story surprised me. It is, indeed, vintage Rule in the easy handling of language, the dead-on accuracy of its speech and the quick penetration of human motives and verbal smoke-screens. But the sheer buoyancy of its humour — albeit black or funereal grey — is a fresh harvest from this author. *Blessed Are The Dead* leaves one laughing and smarting at one and the same time and that, after all, is itself a neat and honest summary of Vancouver life.

Finally there is my own offering, here in that my publisher insisted on it. Blackberries and peace marches are basic ingredients of the Vancouver summer confection for me. Yet I hankered to analyse a recipe rather than just to celebrate a taste. But to dig down to psychological and spiritual compulsions is not, I assert, to invalidate the objective goal or aspiration. This is still Peace City — even if the slogans for an eirenic dream of a nuclear-free world are shouted from the raucous throats of warring couples, from the bored and the under- and un-employed. Vancouver is one hundred years old but it is also a century young. These combined pages of The Vancouver Fiction Book often demonstrate it can by cynical; I wanted my story, as postscript, to suggest it is also often innocent.

— *David Watmough*

HUBERT EVANS was born in 1892 and is thus the most venerable of our contributors. He grew up in Galt, Ontario, and after W.W. 1 service in the Canadian Army he came to dwell in British Columbia. He is the author of twelve books in all and numerous uncollected short stories; his most recently published fiction was the autobiographical novel, *O Time In Your Flight*, in 1979. In later life there have also appeared from his pen the poetry volumes *Whittlings* (1976), and *Endings*, in 1981.

HUBERT EVANS

an excerpt from the novel

The New Front Line

Hugh Henderson stood at the dining room window looking out into the rectangle of prim lawn enclosed by the laurel hedge. It had rained during the night, but now the sun was launching jovial shafts between the houses on the opposite side of the street and co-operating with the recent shower to make the world smell as young and thriving as a greenhouse. A pert robin, like a gentleman farmer with vest pulled down snugly and hands under his slate-grey coattails, inspected his orderly estate of lawn. A milk wagon, with its top still wet from the rain, rolled down the asphalted street to the thin chime of bottles and the honest clop-clopping of hoofs. On the opposite sidewalk a ten-year-old girl in blue and grey jersey, kilted skirt, and worsted stockings, raced her scooter with the milk team. Her bare knees and black, bobbed hair caught the sunlight where it angled between the houses. Her swinging leg sent the scooter onward in short, strong surges. She was a modern picture that might have been called "Child Coursing to Welcome the Day".

It was one of those April mornings in Vancouver when many young hearts — some of them in bodies upon which the jostling years have left their marks — feel a tugging desire to veer skittishly from the shafts of duty and with chins ridiculously high, march on to some outdoor place to help install the spring.

The lengthening newspaper columns headed "Help Wanted" and "Situations Wanted" testified to the radical promptings of that British Columbia spring. Even Hugh's mother had not escaped. For the first time that year she had opened one of the dining-room windows before breakfast. But to conciliate the conservative side of her nature she had qualified the open window by a brisk blaze in the dining-room fireplace.

"Father'll be down in a minute," she said from the kitchen doorway. "You're starving, I know."

"Just comfortably hungry. It looks as if the rain might hold off for a while now," he said, turning from the window.

"I do hope it stays fine. You can't count on the weather here. You'll see it's not a bit like Ontario. What they put the 'probs' in the papers here for, I don't know. They're mostly wrong, at least it seems so. Breakfast's right ready, dear. If you like you might start the toaster."

Hugh switched on the toaster and stood a snowy square of bread upright on either side. The blue and white china, the spotless cloth and polished silver still made him feel that the table belonged in a department store window, and that real food and real people seated about it were not intended to be part of the display. It was one week this morning since he had arrived from Toronto, where his battalion had been demobilized. Previous to that, for three and a half years, he had taken nearly all his meals from a mess-tin. He still clung to the belief that for certain of the more elusive foods, a mess-tin had advantages over the civilian plate with its shelving sides.

As he turned from the table he heard his father on the stairs. His mother came from the kitchen with three plates of porridge. His father, as far back as Hugh could remember, had believed in porridge, in spite of what the breakfast food advertisements might infer. Porridge was an institution in the Henderson household. Grandfather Henderson would as soon have thought of voting against his party as of a breakfast without it, and though Hugh's father had been known to break the family political tradition he remained loyal to porridge. He considered it as Canadian as maple syrup and corn on the cob.

The three Hendersons sat down. Mrs. Henderson recited the time-honoured grace, "O Lord, for what we are about to receive make us truly thankful." While he had been living at home Hugh had never analysed it, but now he had a passing curiosity about what the Lord thought of people who depended

on Him for food and then asked Him for the thankfulness with which to acknowledge it. While the polite supplication was being offered, Henderson senior, with bowed head, slipped his napkin from its ring and spread it over his knees, and when he heard the soft "Amen", he reached for the cream pitcher.

"You beat me down this morning, eh?" he said to Hugh.

"I wasn't roaming the town until after midnight. I'm beginning to think Vancouver's played havoc with your morals, Dad. What would the folks on Maple Avenue, back home, think if they heard their esteemed neighbour rolling home late? And in a taxi, too."

"That doesn't often happen, Hugh," Mrs. Henderson said quickly. Hugh had never joked with his father like this before he went away.

James Henderson's mouth was rather full for laughter, but his face beamed. He knew that Hugh knew he had been down to the hotel to talk with "a party" who might be placing a good order for plate glass one of these days and who, if handled the right way, might place it with the firm he represented.

"That's right, May," he said. "Don't let him get away with that." His face was round, and only for the strength of his mouth and his direct, intent eyes, one might have called him chubby.

"Better come with me this morning," he continued. "We'll lunch downtown, Mother. Got to show him round a bit before he gets back into harness. That right, Hugh?"

Hugh said nothing.

The two men moved out to the hall and took their hats. "There'll be a load of wood up this afternoon, May," he said as they went out. "If you've plans for the afternoon I'll see about paying."

"I'll be home all day." She watched them through the gate. What a fine pair they made. Hugh was as broad shouldered as his father now.

* * * * *

If there had been a deliberate attempt to undermine the united strength of the returned soldiers, it could scarcely have been done more effectively than by fostering some of the so-called soldiers' clubs which blossomed briefly in the spring and summer of 1919 in many Canadian cities and towns, and which kept men from joining one of the worth-while organizations. They soon disbanded, leaving many of their members disgusted with all attempts of the real clubs and associations to aid the veterans.

As Hugh neared a busy corner a jaunty youth in uniform with a pinched-out cigarette behind his ear sidled out from the wall to intercept him. "Say Mac," he began, glancing at Hugh's returned soldier button, "We'd be glad to have you in our outfit."

"What's yours?"

"The Gravel Crushers. Our club room's just round the corner. We got a good bunch of guys. Better come and look us over."

Hugh had no intention of joining the Gravel Crushers but out of curiosity he went. The scout turned into an unswept passage and led him up a flight of stairs into a long bare room. Most of the tables were empty but near the frosted window a noisy group had gathered. The scout took him to the far end of the room where there was an unpainted board partition and a short counter.

"Where's Sid?" he asked the steward. The steward wore a soiled white apron and over his forehead was the curve of hair carefully laid in place with water and a comb, which only bartenders of the old school, divinity students, and the makers of toupees can accomplish.

"Out," said the steward.

"When'll he be in?"

"Search me."

"Look," said the scout confidingly to Hugh, "You stick around. The pres'dent'll be back soon. Make yourself at home. I got to go. Tell him you come in with me."

"Beer?" asked the steward when the youth had gone.

Hugh nodded, took his glass of foam with what beer lay below and started for a table. As he went down the room a man slouching in a chair gazed fixedly up at him and caught his sleeve. "Sit down," he said with a heavy dazed grin. "I want to talk to somebody."

"Better let me make a real drink of that," he went on, fumbling in his hip pocket. He brought out a small bottle and when Hugh declined his offer, he poured all its contents into his own glass and dropped the bottle to the floor. He gulped half the glass, shuddered and grinned wanly. "Hot stuff, boy. That'll make the birdies sing. Got a job yet?"

"Not yet."

"I got one — logging — up the coast. But I won't have the brains to go to it till my blood money's gone. Great life, eh?" He drained his glass and shoved it from him.

"Listen to that gang over in the corner. Think they're back in the estaminet. Soon they'll start dipping their fingers in their beer and drawing maps of the trenches on the table." He turned uncertainly and glared at them. "They don't know the war's over," he confided to Hugh.

As Hugh went down the unswept stairs a husky baritone in the corner of the room was singing the trench parody of "Sing Me to Sleep":

"Far, far from Eee-pray, I want to be
Where German whizzbangs cannot get me
C-o-l-d is my dugout, wet are my feet
Nothing — "

The singing ceased as if the vigilant steward with the curl had intervened.

Hugh continued his walk down the street. Frequently on the lapels of passersby he saw the copper button with its Union Jack shield encircled with the words "For Service at the Front". Some of its wearers were young men, some middle aged, one, a bank messenger in braided uniform, was old. The

Canadian army was being disbanded, its members turning to their peace time work, clerking in stores, operating street cars, in offices, driving trucks, delivering mail, policing the streets; some like himself idling, undecided what they wanted to do; and back there in the Gravel Crushers' club room a shabby little remnant drinking and talking of the old days.

Coming toward him he saw a tanned face. There was old Sandy Biggs, grinning and showing his gold teeth, those teeth which had made him a personage in the eyes of the mesdames of Bruay and the three hamlets of Servin. They greeted each other with the shocking endearments only close male friends dare use.

"When'd you get back, Packy? A week today? Gosh, you're looking good." Biggs and his old platoon-mate edged toward the curb. For almost a year they had been cronies, then Biggs had gone down the line with shrapnel in his thigh and the Armistice had sent him home to Canada instead of to France. "Landed a job yet?"

"Not yet."

"Lots of time. Line 'em up and look 'em over."

"You still have the store up country?"

"Sure. Hard graft on the wife though. But things are looking up. Hacked ties last winter and made enough to get a truck. I'm hauling shingle bolts for the mill now. Things are pretty good in Cedar City. Better come up and start a crown and anchor game." They laughed at that and a youth in a pinch-back suit and pointed shoes who was passing turned to look at them.

"I'd like to come up and have some fishing, Sandy. But I'll have to hustle for a job instead."

"Say, why don't you? I'm going back tomorrow morning. You better come along."

"I'm afraid not. But you come on up to the house for dinner tonight."

"I don't know, Packy. I'm only down for a couple of days, dickering for some stuff I got to get. I didn't bring a clean collar or anything. Some other time, maybe.'' Hugh could see he wanted to accept, and with a little more urging he did. ''Meet you at this corner at what time say? Five o'clock? Right you are.''

* * * * *

Mrs. Henderson was pleased when Hugh telephoned her he was bringing Sandy Biggs home to dinner. In some of his overseas letters Hugh had spoken of Biggs as one of his intimate friends. She knew he was older than Hugh, that he was married and that, though his parents were English, he had been born in British Columbia. Being of pioneer stock herself — her people had been United Empire Loyalists — she thought well of all old pioneer families. ''There was something about them,'' she sometimes said. Never to others and probably never even to herself had she defined this ''something'', but it was evidently to be cherished by those who had it and coveted by those who had not.

* * * * *

During the evening James Henderson encouraged Biggs to talk of Cedar City. Except for a few of the larger centres of population, he knew very little about British Columbia and he did not often have the opportunity to gather first-hand information about it. He asked about the mill, what the settlers were like, what it cost to clear land and similar matters.

''And in your experience what type of people do you find best suited for pioneering? I mean as to nationality and so on.''

''Any kind that's not scared by hard work,'' Biggs grinned. ''Nationality doesn't seem to figure much.''

''A stout heart is essential of course — ''

''That and a strong back. And they got to be handy.''

''It was certainly like that in the old days. I remember when I was a lad on the farm — that's almost fifty years ago — my father used to say that in his younger days they bought no furniture, wagons and such things. They made them. It was slow work, but they got along. They lived simply but they never lacked the essentials.''

Biggs nodded genially. "Up our way I can't say we see more meal times than we do meals. We live good, you bet."

"You and your wife have the store," Mrs. Henderson put in. "But real pioneering — clearing land and such-like — it's all a hard life for a woman."

Hugh, thinking of Biggs, tried to divert the conversation into other channels. He knew what his parents did not — that though Biggs kept a store and took contracts to cut poles, shingle bolts and ties, he was a settler with forty acres of uncleared land. He managed to turn the talk to the excellent fishing and hunting to be had near Cedar City. Biggs told them of trout and deer and bears and when he rose to go he invited them to come up sometime during the summer. "There's some fine sand beaches on the lake, if you like swimming. You should come up and see our country."

"I suppose it's very much like Muskoka," Mrs. Henderson said, "and I did so enjoy our summers there."

When Hugh went upstairs to his room he could hear the soft rain on the young maple leaves outside his windows. He switched off the light and lay on the bed. His thoughts, roaming the winding trails of memory, came finally to a recollection of the last full day he and Sandy Biggs had spent together.

It was in France one March when their battalion was far behind the line on corps rest. He had walked all day with Sandy through a country at that time unscarred by war. They had gone for six kilometres along a cobbled road, looking for a lift from friendly motor lorries, dodging insolent Air Force trucks, saluting with a hollow heartiness staff cars going nowhere in a great hurry. At noon they had stopped at a group of buildings, consisting of a gaunt church, some farm houses with intrusive manure heaps before their doors, and an estaminet. At the estaminet they had asked madame for coffee and French-fried potatoes.

After lunch they went into a sunken road that led upward between hedges to a wooded hill, much frequented, it was said, by correspondents who officially eye-witnessed the minor engagements of that sector.

Hugh remembered vividly all that had happened on that day. There were weeks in France of which he could recall but the barest details. Yet for that one day's leave he could account for his thoughts, for all he said and did. It seemed as if he had been thrashing about in dense mist-wrapped thickets and suddenly had come out upon a knoll from which he could see all about him.

He remembered the shy promise of spring the sunlight gave, and the dun background of the fields through the faint green filigree of the hedges containing the road; the spiritless face of the curé they had met before the church, and how insipidly a little bell had tinkled on the arched collar of a farm horse they passed on the cobbled road.

He and Sandy had cleared the end of the road and mounted through tilted fields to the wood on the top of the hill. Small pines stood there at regular intervals, cone-shaped and symmetrical like Christmas trees upon a stage. The precision of shape and arrangement had depressed him. The rows were a set distance apart and each tree the same distance from its neighbour, so that no matter where you went in that little wood, you were at the intersection of two avenues exactly alike. There could be no surprises in a wood like that.

"Why didn't they juggle them around a bit?" he asked Biggs.

"Search me," Biggs replied. He was lying on his stomach trying to blow sparks from the wick of his cigarette lighter down an ant hill. At that moment he succeeded, then seeing the ants were likely to destroy themselves in trying to remove it, he had plucked it out and burnt his thumb. Then he rolled onto his back and became unresponsive. And finally Hugh forgot the artificiality of the trees' arrangement and let the warm odour of the woods and the sunlight waft him into a pleasant doze.

He turned over on his bed. Was there something symbolic about those trees? He remembered their dreary orderliness, the bleak certainty you could never find one different from the rest. Supposing one of them had grown different from the others, would the methodical forester who planted them come and try to curb its growth? These pioneer ancestors his father had talked about tonight hadn't been bound by a desire for security, hadn't been afraid to go into new places and leave old homes and the ordered lives of others. Some had failed and gone down, no doubt, but others had taken root and flourished in the new soil. There on that hill in France every tree had been no higher or shorter than those all about it. Was the fibre of such timber as tough, he wondered, as that of trees which reared themselves on untended ground and withstood the elements? He liked to think it was not.

The shower became heavier. He heard the murmur of the rain's fingers stroking down the new leaves. The bed-linen was soothing, the war was over, and he was safely home. After four years he was again faced by the old problem of choosing a career.

* * * * *

Hugh had been home about two weeks when his mother had the Mottons to dinner. Perry Motton was in business in the city, and his eldest sister, the matron of the Grayford hospital, was visiting him during her vacation. James Henderson was out of town. "Unless she's reformed, you'll get an earful of gossip," he told Hugh that morning. But his wife looked forward to the evening. Lucy Motton would have so much to tell her, things that had not been written up in the *Weekly Messenger*. Though Mrs. Henderson had left it, she hoped she would always be loyal to Grayford.

"I say, Hugh," Perry said after dinner, "if you're not with anyone yet, it might be worth-while to interview Mr. Hopven, our sales manager. You'd like him. He's enlarging the sales force all the time. You'd find the Flagg-Peasley Corporation awfully decent people."

"What's the line?"

"Oh, you know — confectionary — juvenile specialties.

The demand's growing all the time and our people are meeting it in a big way. They do give a generous commission, besides salary."

"It sounds interesting," Hugh said, but Perry could see he was not enthusiastic.

"It's surprising the business we're doing. We're new in the field here but we're making the other firms hustle. We turn out a high grade article. The kiddies are clever buyers — you can't fool them. Time after time I've watched them come into a store with their nickels and dimes. Once they spot our goods they want them. We're selling ourselves to the kiddies, Hugh. The firm does a lot of high class advertising, too. That helps all of us tremendously."

Hugh found his attention wandering to the talk across the room. "And then, my dear," Miss Motton was saying, "no sooner did I get that case fixed up than what should come in but a strangulated hernia. There we were, two nurses short —" Hugh could see by his mother's face that for all she knew the intruder might have been one of the oddly-named foreigners from the brass foundry. They were always fighting.

"I believe you'd get on well," Motton was saying, "Mr. Hopven is doing all he possibly can for the returned fellows. There's another thing, Hugh. You'd find the service button a wonderful asset. Honestly, it would surprise you the selling pull it has."

That night after the Mottons had gone he asked: "How'd you like to see me forging ahead in the juvenile candy business, Mother? Getting the kids' nickels, big turn-over, good commission. The Flagg-Peasley people are awfully decent."

"Is that what Perry said?"

"Yes. And the button would be a big asset. Gosh, he hasn't changed a bit."

"No, Hugh, I can't say I'd care to see you in that business. It hardly seems — dignified, does it? Perry seems to be doing well. Lucy says he's planning to be married. He's making payments on a bungalow."

Mrs. Henderson did not care to see Hugh on the selling force of the Flagg-Peasley Corporation, but, as the days slipped into weeks and he had not settled down in some line of work, she became vaguely uneasy.

One evening late in April she spoke to her husband about it. They were alone in the house. Mr. Henderson sat reading a trade journal and enjoying his after-dinner cigar. He knew by the way she moved about the living room that something was worrying her. Usually in the evenings she sewed or, in recent years, knitted. She had never found quiet comfort in reading. One of the window shades was a few inches lower than those on either side of it. She went softly and raised it. She tweaked a dead shoot from the fern in the bay window, and straightened one of the leather-covered books on the little table.

"What's the matter, May?" he asked without looking up.

"Have you noticed — it may be my imagination — but Hugh doesn't seem contented."

James Henderson laid his paper across his knees. "Yes, I've noticed. But don't worry. He'll settle down."

"He seemed so happy the first few days he was home. I wish he would settle down. When he went into the store you said the same thing, but he never took to it, you know. I sometimes think he was glad when the war came along and he could get away."

"Oh, he'll come round. It takes time."

"But he seems to be getting less satisfied. He'll soon be twenty-five."

"I know," he admitted.

"James, I sometimes think he'd have gone on to college if we'd encouraged him more."

"Encouraged? He knew we'd see him through."

"Doesn't it seem a pity he didn't? There was that Bennett boy so anxious to go that he worked his way through. Hugh wouldn't have had to do that. I'm sure he'd have liked it, once he made a start."

"Perhaps, but there's no cause to worry. He'll do well in

business. And the professions are overcrowded. In business there's always room at the top. He's not the slap-dash kind. Even if he is a little headstrong that'll help him later on. He's not easily discouraged."

"I wish he'd make a start right away."

"Yes, the sooner he's into something full swing, the sooner he'll be happy. He's more or less in the air now. Once he gets something this restlessness will disappear. I'm keeping my eye open for the first thing that turns up."

"Of course it's natural for him to be unsettled after the war. I'm over-anxious for him, I suppose."

* * * * *

By the end of April Hugh realized he had reached a crisis. Unless he was going to drift all his life he must have it out with the old problem of what he was going to do. During the years he was overseas he had scarcely given it a thought. There, speculation on the future was simplified. If you were killed, thinking about it would be so much time wasted. If you weren't, that glorious fact was sufficient. From Halifax to Vancouver, Canada had its tens of thousands like him in those after-the-war days. They had enlisted as youths, who in the early days of the war were just feeling their way into a vocation of some kind. During the years they were overseas their younger brothers had marched on, occupied the positions they had left, then advanced to more important ones. The gaps had been closed and the returned men who had gone out from Canada as youths must either take their places at the foot of the line or crowd out civilians younger than themselves. The aggressive crowded, the others submitted. Hugh was not submissive and had he seen a place he wanted few would have jostled harder than he. But there was the difficulty. He saw no place he wanted.

Some returned men he knew were resuming their interrupted university studies. They were attending lectures with young men and women who had been children when the war broke out. Hugh knew his parents would finance him if he wanted to go to University. But he was too honest to accept financial aid when he knew he would not take full advantage of the opportunity, and he thought he had not the qualifications for a student.

Almost everyone he had known before the war who did not go to university went into business. Business had little appeal for him.

He asked himself if he was too particular. These others, — his father, and the thousands of men like them, — what justification had he for assuming they were perpetually satisfied with the work they did day after day? Perhaps they too had secret hopes of living life exactly as they wanted to, but when they found they couldn't they took the next best thing. Life was a rough-and-tumble affair. These men were sportsmen; they took the knocks, accepted the handicaps, and kept on playing so heartily that spectators like himself were fooled into thinking they enjoyed every minute of the game. Perhaps when they were off the field, out of sight, some of them asked themselves what the game was all about.

What the game was all about! It was that which puzzled him. It wasn't that he didn't want to join in; he did. He longed to take a header into this rugby game of life, to glory in the crashing tackles, the slow gains, the hard-fought losses. But this game of business confused him. He felt he could never understand it well enough to be deeply roused by it. And any game he played he wanted to play hard. If only he could find the sort of game for which he was suited!

One Sunday afternoon he and his father went to the park for a walk. They went to the bear cages and joined the crowd of city people making Sabbath offerings of peanuts to those demigods of the great outdoors. They looked up at the mountain goats waggling their chin whiskers at the crowd, they watched the monkeys perform their comic-strip antics, and they were fortunate enough to be present when the kangaroo actually hopped.

Hundreds of people strolled over the sloping lawns. They

saw a middle-aged Japanese man wearing the first straw hat of the season. His wife in snowy shirtwaist and trailing skirt walked with him. Her high glossy pompadour shone in the sunlight. Her narrow eyes below the interrogative brows were politely pleased. Their chromatic scale of children had been scoured and polished. Farther to the left, in the children's playground, each swing and its occupant was a pendulum ticking off the precious seconds of an afternoon of pleasure. Three turbaned Sikhs with heavy yellow walking-sticks paraded.

Hugh and his father turned into the pavilion for sandwiches and lemonade. From the balcony they looked over the lawns and playgrounds.

"Do you think you'll like Vancouver, Hugh?" his father asked. "How does it strike you as a place to settle down?"

"I like it well enough as a city. But as a place to settle down — well that doesn't appeal much to me just now. I'm fed up with loafing though. I'm almost ready to take the first thing that comes along."

"That's the right spirit, but we don't want to be too hasty. There are jobs and jobs. Getting into the swing of things won't be easy. But the best way to forget about the war is to get into something that interests you."

"I guess you're right."

"Tell me, Hugh, have you ever changed your mind about college? If you want to go, your mother and I are behind you. We'll see you through."

"Thanks. But I've thought about it and decided not to."

James Henderson shoved his glass aside and leaned slightly forward. "All right. You'll be coming into business then."

Hugh looked up quickly. "Oh, I don't know about business. There must be other things. I was no whirlwind in the store, you know."

"MacIsaacs always spoke well enough of your work. And if you don't want to follow business or a profession what else is there that you'd want?"

''Lots of things. There are jobs outside the city, up the coast or back in the mountains somewhere.''

James Henderson looked at his son. ''It's the outdoor life that makes you think of them. I'm as fond of the outdoors as you are, Hugh, but a man must look ahead. Scenery and fishing and hunting don't put much into your bank account. You cannot jeopardize your career for things like that. My advice is, stay in the city. That's where the big money is. And once you have the money you can have these other things if you want them.''

Hugh did not reply and he went on, ''Your mother and I are confident that once you get started you'll make good. All of us find it difficult to choose just the career we want. For some reason it's been particularly hard for you. But you've got the right stuff in you. You'll be all right.''

''Certainly I don't want to let you and mother down. Whatever I start I want to succeed at. I do like the outdoors and it seems to me you can't be a real success unless you're happy at your job. After all, surroundings should be considered, shouldn't they?''

''I can't agree.'' The unintentional severity of those words transformed their conversation to an argument on ethics and a creed of living. James Henderson had escaped in youth from the uncompromising discipline of a narrow religious belief. The ploughs of a widened experience had torn away practically all of its teachings but a few tough roots remained. ''No, I cannot agree,'' he repeated.

''I don't think you should let personal like or dislike of surroundings have anything to do with the choice of a career, Hugh.'' The severity had gone from his voice. In Hugh's eyes he saw that determination which sometimes made him difficult to manage as a boy. ''I think it is up to everyone to take full advantage of his opportunities, and I don't believe that pleasure should have much to do with it. That is, any more than the pleasure we get in a hard job well done!''

"Perhaps I'm too fussy," Hugh conceded, though he could not feel that his father was right.

* * * * *

In their room that night James Henderson told his wife something of his talk with Hugh in the park. He did not tell her everything because he had long ago learned that she looked upon serious discussion as argument and all arguments distressed her.

"I think we'll see Hugh settling down soon," he said.

Mrs. Henderson's slight figure turned away from her mirror toward him. "Here? In Vancouver?" she asked quickly. The skilful fingers on her hair stopped plaiting, as if they too were eager for the answer.

"Oh yes. He seems to like Vancouver."

The fingers on the braid danced. "I'm so glad. When will he start?"

"As soon as he gets something worth-while. I've my eye on something that will suit him."

"Did you tell him that?"

"Not yet, but I will."

Mrs. Henderson waited, hoping he would tell her more.

"He wants to get back into harness as quickly as possible. He's tired of loafing he says. I renewed our offer about college but he doesn't want that."

"James — I — sometimes I don't care what he does, if only I know he's happy."

"He's wise in getting down to business at once," her husband concluded as he got heavily into bed. "Competition's keen these days. One thing about Hugh he's not afraid of hard work and I know he'll come to like the game."

For a long time after the light had been snapped out Mrs. Henderson lay awake thinking of her son.

During the first days he was at home, when her eager affection made her want him always within sight, within touch of her hand, she was forced to see that he had changed. In those three and a half years he had been away something had happened. It was as if she stood close to him again but that between them a thin crystal curtain had been lowered. She recognized and took joy in the sound of his voice, his old familiar gestures, the thousand little mannerisms which were always his, yet that separating curtain had robbed her of that feeling of contact, had insulated her from the radiation of his personality which had warmed her heart before he went overseas. She tried to find assurance in thinking she only imagined this change.

More than ever she did little things for him, little intimate things, as if by trying to create a dependence on her she could turn back the years and recover what they had taken.

Now in her bed, her thin hands on the bedcovers, her fingers nervously picking at the end of her braid, and the house so dark and silent, she was planning ways to make Hugh's room more attractive. He could use the front bedroom as a den. A wicker reading lamp with yellow silk lining and some of that pretty cretonne she had seen would be nice. He would like the big rose splashes and the black spots, would think it cheerful without being too frivolous. And she would have the two old armchairs done over in leatherette. It was going to be wonderful now it was practically decided he would not go away.

* * * * *

In his bedroom down the hall Hugh was awake. A ridiculous fancy had formed itself in his mind. On the stage of his thoughts two ideas were wrangling. One idea kept saying, "Cut loose and do what you feel like doing." . . . "Be practical," the other urged. "Don't chuck away your chances." . . . And an impish voice off-stage interrupted the dialogue . . . "It's a curse to be an only child," it kept insisting. "If you had some brothers you'd have a chance of doing what you liked. You could roam and do what you wanted to. They'd have others and they wouldn't interfere so with your life. But you can't do what you want to. . . . You can't. . . . You can't. You're an only child and they'll hang onto you. They'll coddle you. Too bad, of course, but they will."

ETHEL WILSON was born in Port Elizabeth, South Africa and died in Vancouver in 1980 aged ninety-two. She came to Canada when she was only ten and this city was her home for much of her long life. She was a late-developer as a writer but from the 1930s when she published her first stories in *The New Statesman & Nation* she produced six volumes of fiction including *Swamp Angel, The Innocent Traveller*, and *Mrs. Golightly & Other Stories.*

ETHEL WILSON

Down at English Bay

Once upon a time there was a negro who lived in Vancouver and his name was Joe Fortes. He lived in a small house by the beach at English Bay and there is now a little bronze plaque to honour and memory near-by, and he taught hundreds of little boys and girls how to swim. First of all he taught them for the love of it and after that he was paid a small salary by the City Council or the Parks Board, but he taught for love just the same. And so it is that there are Judges, and Aldermen, and Cabinet Ministers, and lawyers, and doctors, and magnates, and ordinary businessmen, and grandmothers, and prostitutes, and burglars, and Sunday School superintendents, and dry-cleaners, and so on whom Joe Fortes taught to swim, and they will be the first to admit it. And Joe Fortes saved several people from drowning; some of them were worth saving and some were not worth saving in the slightest — take the man who was hanged in Kingston jail; but Joe Fortes could not be expected to know this, so he saved everyone regardless. He was greatly beloved and he was respected.

Joe Fortes was always surrounded by little boys and girls in queer bathing suits in the summer-time. The little boys' bathing suits had arms and legs not to speak of bodies and almost skirts on them; and the little girls were covered from neck to calf in blue serge or alpaca with white braid — rows of it — round the sailor collar and the full skirt, and a good pair of black wool stockings. This all helped to weigh them down when they tried to learn to swim, and to drown the little girls, in particular, when possible.

Joe had a nice round brown face and a beautiful brown body and arms and legs as he waded majestically in the waves of

English Bay amongst all the little white lawyers and doctors and trained nurses and seamstresses who jumped up and down and splashed round him. "Joe," they called, and "Look at me, Joe! Is this the way?" and they splashed and swallowed and Joe supported them under their chins and by their behinds and said in his rich slow fruity voice, "Kick out, naow! Thassa-way. Kick right out!" And sometimes he supported them, swimming like frogs, to the raft, and when they had clambered on to the raft they were afraid to jump off and Joe Fortes became impatient and terrible and said in a very large voice, "Jump now! I'll catch you! You jump off that raff or I'll leave you here all night!" And that was how they learned to swim.

Rose was one of the children who learned to swim with Joe Fortes, and she was one of the cowardly ones who shivered on the raft while Joe roared, "You jump off of that raff this minute, or I'll leave you there all night!" So she jumped because the prospect was so terrible and so real, and how threatening the wet sea by night, and who knows what creatures will come to this dark raft alone. So she jumped.

Aunt Rachel did not let Rose go swimming in her good blue serge bathing costume with white braid and black wool stockings unless some grown-up was there. Aunts and guardians feel much more responsible for children than parents do, and so they are over-anxious and they age faster. Aunt Topaz was not very much good as a guardian because she did not bathe, could not swim, was irresponsible, and usually met friends on the beach with whom she entered into conversation and then forgot about Rose.

One day, however, Rose persuaded her Aunt Rachel to let her go to the beach with Aunt Topaz who was quite ready for an outing, and in any case wanted to take her bicycle for a walk. So Rose and her Great-Aunt started off down Barclay Street in very good spirits on a sunny July afternoon. Tra-la-la, how happy they were! They talked separately and together. Aunt Topaz wheeled her bicycle, which gave her a very sporting appearance, and she wore her hat which looked like a row-boat.

She carried some biscuits in the string bag which was attached to the shining handle-bars of her noble English bicycle. Rose carried a huge parcel in a towel and swung it by a strap. She further complicated her walk by taking her hoop and stick. So Great-Aunt and Great-Neice proceeded down Barclay Street towards English Bay, Rose bowling her hoop whenever she felt like it.

When they arrived at English Bay Rose rushed into the bath-house with five cents, and Aunt Topaz got into conversation with a young man called Eustace Flowerdew, with whose mother she was acquainted. Eustace Flowerdew wore a stiff straw hat attached to him somewhere by a black cord, so that if in his progress along the sands the hat should blow off, if would still remain attached to the person of Eustace. He wore pince-nez which made him look very refined. His collar was so high and stiff that it hurt him, and his tie was a chaste and severe four-in -hand. He collected tie-pins which were called stick-pins. Today he wore a stick-pin with the head of a horse.

"Oh, good afternoon, Eustace," said Aunt Topaz, "how nice you do look to be sure. How is your mother what a nice horse!"

After taking off his hat and putting it on again, Eustace hitched up each of his trouser legs and sat down beside Aunt Topaz, and looked over the top of his collar. In so doing he jiggled the bicycle which was unusually heavy and was in - expertly propped against the log on which he and Aunt Topaz were sitting. The bicycle intentionally fell on them both and knocked them down. This bicycle was very ill-tempered and ingenious, and was given to doing this kind of thing when possible on purpose. Aunt Topaz lay prone, and Eustace Flowerdew crawled out and lifted the bicycle off her and led it away to a tree where it could not touch them any more. Aunt Topaz exclaimed a great deal, got up, dusted the sand off herself, and Rose was as forgotten as though she had never existed.

"What are you doing on the beach at this time of the afternoon, Eustace?" asked Aunt Topaz.

Eustace did not want to tell Aunt Topaz the truth, which was that he hoped to meet a girl called Mary Evans in whom he had become interested, so he told her a lie.

"I have come here to forget, Miss Edgeworth," he said, looking at the ocean over his collar.

"And what do you want to forget? . . . Oh, I suppose I shouldn't ask you if you want to forget it! How very interesting!"

The young man took his hat off and passed his hand over his forehead wearily. "He is good-looking, but he looks rather silly," thought Topaz.

"The fact is that I am writing a play," he said at last.

Topaz was frightfully excited. She had never before sat on a log with someone who was writing a play. Memories of Sir Henry Irving, Ellen Terry and the Lyceum Theatre in general romped through her mind and she did not know where to begin. She bubbled a little but the young man did not seem to hear. He was still looking out to sea. How beautiful it was, beyond the cries and splashings of children who crowded round Joe Fortes. There is a serenity and a symmetry about English Bay. It is framed by two harmonious landfalls. Out stretches Point Grey sloping to the south-west. Undulations of mountain, manland, and island come to a poetic termination on the north-west. Straight ahead to the westward sparkles the ocean as far as the dim white peaks of Vancouver Island. Sea-gulls flash and fry and cry in the wide summer air. Sitters on the beach regarded this beauty idly.

"What are you calling your play, Eustace?" asked Aunty when she had recovered.

"*Break, Break, Break,*" said the young man. "Who is this uncommonly plain little girl standing in front of us? How very wet she is!"

"That?" said Aunt Topaz, suddenly seeing Rose. "Oh, there you are. How do you do, Rose? That is my great-niece. Yes, she is plain, isn't she? When wet. When dry she looks better, because her hair curls. Now run away and enjoy yourself and make sure you don't drown. Well, what is it?''

''May I get a biscuit?'' asked Rose, who had come up full of rapture and talk now quenched.

''Yes, yes. Get a biscuit but be careful of the bicycle. It's against that tree.''

Rose looked hatingly at Eustace Flowerdew and went over to the bicycle, dripping as she went. No sooner did she touch the heavy bicycle than it rushed violently away from her down the beach and hurled itself into the sand where it lay with its pedals quivering. Rose looked, but the two had not seen this. So she went and pulled up the bicycle and led it over to the tree again. She propped it up against the tree as best she could, dusted some of the sand off the biscuits, ate them grit and all, and ran off again to the heavenly waves and children surrounding Joe Fortes.

''What does your mother say about your writing a play? I should think she would feel very nervous. Are you introducing the sex element at all . . . illicit love, so to speak . . . or are you, if I may say so, keeping it thoroughly wholesome?'' asked Topaz.

''My dear Miss Edgeworth,'' answered the young man pityingly, ''I trust that you do not still regard Art as being in any way connected with morality!'' He saw in the distance a figure that looked like Mary Evans, and his muscles were already flexing to rise. A shadow fell across Aunty and Eustace.

''Well, I do declare!'' exclaimed Aunty joyously. ''If this isn't Mrs. Hamilton Coffin! Mrs. Coffin, let me present to you a rising young . . .'' but the rising young playwright was no longer there. He was striding away down the beach.

''Do sit down, Mrs. Coffin!'' said Topaz. ''This *is* nice! How very athletic you do look!'' She was filled with admiration. Mrs. Coffin was tall and the black serge bathing suit which she wore did not become her. On this fine summer day Mrs. Coffin, warmly dressed for swimming, displayed no part of her body except her face and ears and her arms as far up as her elbows. ''How delightful!'' exclaimed Topaz sincerely.

"I have lately, Miss Edgeworth," said Mrs. Coffin, who was a serious woman, "come under the influence of Ralston's Health Foods, and so has by husband. We are making a careful study of physical health and exercise and right thinking. We eat Ralston's Health Foods and a new food called Grape Nuts" (" 'Grape Nuts!' that sounds delicious!" said Topaz) "twice a day. Already complexion is brighter, our whole mental attitude is improved, and I *may* say," she lowered her voice, "that faulty elimination is corrected."

"Faulty elimation! Well, well! Fancy that!" echoed Aunt Topaz, and wondered "What on earth is she talking about?"

"I have also make an appointment with Mr. Fortes for a swimming lesson and I hope very soon to have mastered the art. This is my third lesson."

"Never too old to learn! Never too old to learn!" said Topaz merrily but without tact. She had no intention of taking swimming lessons herself. "I will come down to the water's edge and cheer you on." "I wonder if it's her costume or her name that makes me think of the tomb," she thought cheerfully.

Mrs. Coffin and Aunt Topaz went down to the water's edge. Joe Fortes disentangled himself from the swimming, bobbing, prancing, screaming children, and came out of the ocean to speak to Mrs. Coffin. He looked very fine, beautiful brown seal that he was, with the clear sparkling water streaming off him.

Mrs. Coffin advanced into the sea, and unhesitatingly dipped herself. "How brave! How brave! Bravo!" cried Topaz from the brink, clapping. Joe Fortes discussed the motions of swimming with Mrs. Coffin, doing *so* with his arms, and then *so* with his big legs like flexible pillars, and Mrs. Coffin took the first position. Joe Fortes respectfully supported her chin with the tips of his strong brown fingers. He dexterously and modestly raised her rear, and held it raised by a bit of bathing suit. "How politely he does it!" thought Topaz, admiring Joe Fortes and Mrs. Coffin as they proceeded up and down the ocean. When Mrs. Coffin had proceeded up and down supported and exhorted by Joe Fortes for twenty minutes or so, with Topaz addressing them from the brink, she tried swimming alone. She went under several times dragged down by her bathing suit but emerged full of hope. She dressed, and came and sat with Aunt Topaz.

"I understand, Miss Edgeworth," said Mrs. Coffin, "that you are the President of the Minerva Club!"

"I! President! Oh dear no!" said Topaz laughing merrily. "Never again will I be President of anything as long as I live! I was for a year President of our Ladies' Aid, and the worry nearly killed me! I'd as soon be hanged as be President of anything — much sooner, I assure you! No, Mrs. Coffin, I am the Secretary of the Minerva Club — Honorary you understand — and Mrs. Aked, the President, promises that I can toss it up! toss it up! at any moment that I wish!"

Mrs. Coffin seemed to be about to say something further when a miserable-looking object appeared in front of them. It was Rose, blue and dripping.

"J-J-oe F-F-Fortes s-s-says that I'm b-b-b-blue and I must g-g-go home," stuttered Rose shivering. "I d-d-d-don't want to. D-D-Do I have to?

"Oh dear me, what a sight!" said Aunt Topaz who had forgotten Rose again. "Certainly, certainly! Rush into your clothes and we'll walk home briskly and have some tea! What a delightful afternoon!"

On the way home the two pushed their impedimenta. Rose took the superfluous hoop, and Aunt Topaz wheeled her bicycle. The bicycle kicked her with its large protruding pedals as often as possible, and became entangled in her long skirt from time to time, so she often had to stop. When she was disentangled they went on. The bicycle bided its time, and then it kicked her again. Their minds were full of their own affairs, of which they talked regardless.

"A very silly young man, I'm afraid, but he may grow out of it. It is possible, however, that he has talent. . . ."

"I swam six strokes alone. I swam six strokes alone. . ."

"I'm sure Mrs. Hamilton Coffin deserves a great deal of

credit at her age. . . ."

"Joe Fortes says that if I can just master the . . ."

"But what she meant by 'faulty elimination' I cannot imagine. It may have something to do with the Mosaic Law. . . ."

"Joe Fortes can swim across English Bay easy-weasy. A big boy said that Joe Fortes could swim across the English Channel easy-weasy . . ."

"I do wish you'd stop saying 'easy-weasy' . . . oh . . ." The bicycle, behaving coarsely, swerved, turned, and tried to run Aunt Topaz down.

"And Geraldine has been swimming longer than me and she can't swim as good as me. . . ."

"As well as I. 'Grape Nuts' sound delicious! A combination of grapes and nuts no doubt. . . ."

This kind of conversation went on all the way home, and after they reached home too, until Rose went to bed. It was plain to Rachel and her mother that Aunty and Rose had enjoyed going down to English Bay, and Rachel was greatly relieved that Rose had not been drowned.

On the next afternoon Aunt Topaz prepared to go to the meeting of the Minerva Club. She dressed very prettily, and wore a feather boa. Her success in dress was a matter of luck rather than taste, but today she looked uncommonly well. "How nice you look, Anty!" said Rachel admiringly. Aunty was very happy. She pranced up Barclay Street, carrying her Minutes of the previous meeting — which were brief — in her hand.

There were nine ladies gathered at Mrs. Aked's house for the meeting of the Minerva Club. Tap, tap went Mrs. Aked on a little table. "We will now call the meeting to order, and our Honorary Secretary will read the Minutes of the previous meeting — Miss Edgeworth."

Everybody admired the experience and aplomb of Mrs. Aked.

Topaz arose and smiled at the ladies. Nine of them. When it came to reading aloud, even Minutes, she enjoyed herself thoroughly. But if she had to utter a single impromptu word in public, on her feet, she suffered more than tongue could tell. Therefore she was careful never to place herself in a position where she might have to make a speech. Considering that she spent her whole life in speaking, this was strange. But human beings are very strange, and there you are.

Topaz reported, smiling over her Minutes, that at the previous meeting the Minerva Club had listened to a paper on Robert Browning and that selections from that great man's less obscure poems had been read aloud. It had been decided that today's meeting should include a brief comprehensive paper on "Poets of the Elizabethan Era" by Mrs. Howard Henchcliffe who certainly had her work cut out, and that selections from the verses of Elizabethan poets would be read by Mrs. Isaacs, Mrs. Simpson, and — modestly — Miss Edgeworth. Then Aunt Topaz sat down. How she enjoyed this!

"Any business, ladies?" enquired Mrs. Aked. "Ah, yes, one vacancy in the Club. The name of Mrs. Hamilton Coffin is up for election. Any discussion before we vote Mrs. Hamilton Coffin into the Club? I think not."

But a rather pudding-faced lady raised a tentative hand. She cleared her throat. "Pardon *me,*" she said. "I hope we are all friends here, and that discussion may be without prejudice?"

Mrs. Aked nodded, and the ladies murmured and rustled and adjusted their boas.

"Before voting on the name of Mrs. Hamilton Coffin," said the pudding-faced lady, "may I remind ladies present that the reputation of our members has always been beyond reproach?"

"I'm sure Mrs. Hamilton Coffin . . ." began a small lady with sparkling eyes, in outraged tones. "Whatever can this be?" wondered Topaz.

The pudding-faced lady again held up her hand. "Pardon *me*," she said, "I have nothing at all to say against the personal reputation of Mrs. Hamilton Coffin. But *do* the Ladies of the Minerva Club know that Mrs. Hamilton Coffin has been seen more than once in a public place, bathing in the arms of a black man?"

A rustle of indignation ran through the room, whether at the pudding-faced lady or at Mrs. Hamilton Coffin it was impossible to say.

Suddenly in that inward part of her that Topaz had not known to exist, arose a fury. She who did not know of the existence of private life because she had no private life of her own, she who feared so greatly to speak in public, she who was never roused to anger, rose to her feet, trembling and angry. She was angry for Joe Fortes; and for Mrs. Hamilton Coffin; and for herself, a spectator on that innocent blue day. She was aware of something evil and stupid in the room.

"Ladies," she said, shaking, "I shall now count ten because I think I shall then be better able to say what I want to say and because I am very frightened. Excuse me just a minute." And Topaz was silent, and they could see her counting ten. All the ladies waited; emotions were held in check. Then the plain and interesting face of Topaz lighted with its usual friendly smile.

"Ladies," she said, "I was present yesterday when that admirable woman Mrs. Hamilton Coffin had her swimming lesson from our respected fellow-citizen Joe Fortes. I know that the lady who has just spoken," and Aunty smiled winningly upon the pudding-faced lady, "will be quite properly relieved to hear that so far from swimming in the arms of Mr. Fortes, which any of us who were drowning would be grateful to do, Mrs. Hamilton Coffin was swimming in his finger-tips. I feel that we should be honoured to have as a fellow-member so active, progressive, and irreproachable a lady as Mrs. Hamilton Coffin. I therefore beg to propose the name of Mrs. Hamilton Coffin as the tenth member of the Minerva Club." And she sat down scarlet-cheeked, shaking violently.

"Hear-hear, hear-hear," said all the ladies — including the pudding-faced lady — with one accord and very loud, clapping. "Order, order," cried the President, enjoying herself immensely. "I hereby declare Mrs. Hamilton Coffin a member of the Minerva Club, and I instruct our Honorary Secretary to write a letter of invitation. I will now call upon Miss Topaz

Edgeworth to read the introductory selection from one of the poets of the Elizabethan Era."

The ladies slipped back their boas and emitted releasing breaths of warm air (the room had become close), adjusted their positions, and adopted postures suitable to those about to listen to the poets.

Aunt Topaz stood and read. This was her great day. How beautifully she read! Her chattering tones were modulated and musical. The training of the classical Mrs. Porter had made Aunty a reader in the classical style. She was correct, deliberate, flowing, unemotional, natural. She was very happy, reading aloud slowly to the Minerva Club. She read clearly —

"Even such is Time, that takes in trust
Our youth, our joys, our all we have,
And pays us but with earth and dust;
Who, in the dark and silent grave,
When we have wandered all our ways,
Shuts up the story of our days.
But from this earth, this grave, this dust,
My God shall raise me up, I trust."

Everybody clapped.

Aunty went home disturbed and happy; and that evening she told her sister and Rachel about the meeting, and her indignation rose and fell and was satisfied. She told it several times.

The Grandmother said, "I am glad you spoke as you did, my dear sister. You were right."

Rachel put down her work. She thought, "How often I am angry with Anty! How often I scold her! She *is* aggravating, but just see this!" Rachel looked across at Aunt Topaz with eyes at once sombre and bright that were Rachel's only beauty. "Yes, Anty," she said, "that's true. I have never heard you say an unkind thing about anyone. I have never heard you cast an aspersion on anyone. I really believe that you are one of the few people who think no evil."

Aunty *was* amazed! Rachel, who seldom praised, had praised her. She — Topaz — who was never humble and embarrassed became humble and embarrassed. What could she say. "I think," she said, "that I will go to bed. I will take the newspaper." And she stumbled upstairs in her hasty way.

Above, in her bedroom they heard her singing in that funny little flute voice of hers.

MALCOLM LOWRY (1909-1957) lived in the Vancouver area from 1937 until 1954, mainly in a beach shack at Dollarton, on the North Shore. This period of seventeen years saw the publication of *Under The Volcano* in 1947. It also produced the experiences reflected in both *October Ferry To Gabriola* and the stories in *Hear Us O Lord From Heaven Thy Dwelling Place* from which we have selected for this anthology.

MALCOLM LOWRY

The Bravest Boat

It was a day of spindrift and blowing sea-foam, with black clouds presaging rain driven over the mountains from the sea by a wild March wind.

But a clean silver sea light came from along the horizon where the sky itself was like glowing silver. And far away over in America the snowy volcanic peak of Mount Hood stood on high, disembodied, cut off from earth, yet much too close, which was an even surer presage of rain, as though the mountains had advanced, or were advancing.

In the park of the seaport the giant trees swayed, and taller than any were the tragic Seven Sisters, a constellation of seven noble red cedars that had grown there for hundreds of years, but were now dying, blasted, with bare peeled tops and stricken boughs. (They were dying rather than live longer near civilization. Yet though everyone had forgotten they were called after the Pleiades and thought they were named with civic pride after the seven daughters of a butcher, who seventy years before when the growing city was named Gaspool had all danced together in a shop window, nobody had the heart to cut them down.)

The angelic wings of the seagulls circling over the tree tops shone very white against the black sky. Fresh snow from the night before lay far down the slopes of the Canadian mountains, whose freezing summits, massed peak behind spire, jaggedly traversed the country northward as far as the eye could reach. And highest of all an eagle, with the poise of a skier, shot endlessly down the world.

In the mirror, reflecting this and much besides, of an old weighing machine with the legend *Your weight and your destiny* encircling its forhead and which stood on the embankment between the streetcar terminus and a hamburger stall, in this mirror along the reedy edge of the stretch of water below known as Lost Lagoon two figures in mackintoshes were approaching, a man and a beautiful passionate-looking girl, both bare-headed, and both extremely fair, and hand-in-hand, so that you would have taken them for young lovers, but that they were alike as brother and sister, and the man, although he walked with youthful nervous speed, now seemed older than the girl.

The man, fine-looking, tall, yet thick-set, very bronzed, and on approaching still closer obviously a good deal older than the girl, and wearing one of those blue belted trenchcoats favored by merchant marine officers of any country, though without any corresponding cap — moreover the trenchcoat was rather too short in the sleeve so that you could see some tattooing on his wrist, as he approached nearer still it seemed to be an anchor — whereas the girl's raincoat was of some sort of entrancing forest-green corduroy — the man paused every now and then to gaze into the lovely laughing face of his girl, and once or twice they both stopped, gulping in great draughts of salty clean sea and mountain air. A child smiled at them, and they smiled back. But the child belonged elsewhere, and the couple were unaccompanied.

In the lagoon swam wild swans, and many wild ducks: mallards and buffleheads and scaups, golden eyes, and cackling black coots with carved ivory bills. The little buffleheads often took flight from the water and some of them blew about like doves among the smaller trees. Under these trees lining the bank other ducks were sitting meekly on the sloping lawn, their beaks tucked into their plumage rumpled by the wind. The smaller trees were apples and hawthorns, some just opening into bloom even before they had foliage, and weeping willows, from whose branches small showers from the night's rain were scattered on the two figures as they passed.

A red-breasted merganser cruised in the lagoon, and at this swift and angry sea bird, with his proud disordered crest, the two were now gazing with a special sympathy, perhaps because he looked lonely without his mate. Ah, they were wrong. The red-breasted merganser was now joined by his wife and on a sudden duck's impulse and with immense fuss the two wild creatures flew off to settle on another part of the lagoon. And for some reason this simple fact appeared to make these two good people — for nearly all people are good who walk in parks — very happy again.

Now at a distance they saw a small boy, accompanied by his father who was kneeling on the bank, trying to sail a toy boat in the lagoon. But the blustery March wind soon slanted the tiny yacht into trouble and the father hauled it back, reaching out with his curved stick, and set it on an upright keel again for his son.

Your weight and your destiny.

Suddenly the girl's face, at close quarters in the weighing machine's mirror, seemed struggling with tears: she unbuttoned the top button of her coat to readjust her scarf, revealing, attached to a gold chain around her neck, a small gold cross. They were quite alone now, standing on top of the embankment by the machine, save for a few old men feeding the ducks below, and the father and his son with the toy yacht, all of whom had their backs turned, while an empty tram abruptly city-bound trundled around the minute terminus square; and the man, who had been trying to light his pipe, took her in his arms and tenderly kissed her, and then pressing his face against her cheek, held her a moment closely.

The couple, having gone down obliquely to the lagoon once more, had now passed the boy with his boat and his father. They were smiling again. Or as much as they could while eating hamburgers. And they were smiling still as they passed the slender reeds where a northwestern redwing was trying to pretend he had no notion of nesting, the northwestern redwing who like all birds in these parts may feel superior to man in that he is his own customs official, and can cross the wild border without let.

Along the far side of Lost Lagoon the green dragons grew thickly, their sheathed and cowled leaves giving off their peculiar animal-like odor. The two lovers were approaching the forest in which, ahead, several footpaths threaded the ancient trees. The park, seagirt, was very large, and like many parks throughout the Pacific Northwest, wisely left in places to the original wilderness. In fact, though its beauty was probably unique, it was quite like some American parks, you might have thought, save for the Union Jack that galloped evermore by a pavilion, and but for the apparition, at this moment, passing by on the carefully landscaped road slightly above, which led with its tunnels and detours to a suspension bridge, of a posse of Royal Canadian Mounted Policemen mounted royally upon the cushions of an American Chevrolet.

Nearer the forest were gardens with sheltered beds of snowdrops and here and there a few crocuses lifting their sweet chalices. The man and his girl now seemed lost in thought, breasting the buffeting wind that blew the girl's scarf out behind her like a pennant and blew the man's thick fair hair about his head.

A loudspeaker. enthroned on a wagon, barked from the city of Enochvilleport composed of dilapidated half-skyscrapers, at different levels, some with all kinds of scrap iron, even broken airplanes, on their roofs, others being moldy stock exchange buildings, new beer parlors crawling with verminous light even in mid-afternoon and resembling gigantic emerald-lit public lavatories for both sexes, masonries containing English teashoppes where your fortune could be told by a female relative of Maximilian of Mexico, totem pole factories, drapers' shops with the best Scotch tweed and opium dens in the basement (though no bars, as if, like some hideous old roué shuddering with every unmentionable secret vice this city without gaiety had cackled "No, I draw the line at that. — What would our wee laddies come to then?"), cerise conflagrations of cinemas, modern apartment buildings, and other soulless behemoths, housing, it might be, noble invisible struggles, of literature, the drama, art or music, the student's lamp and the rejected manuscript; or indescribable poverty and degradation, between which civic attractions were squeezed occasional lovely dark ivy-clad old houses that seemed weeping, cut off from all light, on their knees, and elsewhere bankrupt hospitals, and one or two solid-stoned old banks, held up that afternoon; and among which appeared too, at infrequent intervals, beyond a melancholy never-striking black and white clock that said three, dwarfed spires belonging to frame facades with blackened rose windows, queer grimed onion-shaped domes, and even Chinese pagodas, so that first you thought you were in the Orient, then Turkey or Russia, though finally, but for the fact that some of these were churches, you would be sure you were in hell: despite that anyone who had ever really been in hell must have given Enochvilleport a nod of recognition, further affirmed by the spectacle, at first not unpicturesque, of the numerous sawmills relentlessly smoking and champing away like demons, Molochs fed by whole mountainsides of forests that never grew again, or by trees that made way for grinning regiments of villas in the background of "our expanding and fair city," mills that shook the very earth with their tumult, filling the windy air with their sound as of a wailing and gnashing of teeth: all these curious achievements of man, together creating as we say "the jewel of the Pacific," went as though down a great incline to a harbor more spectacular than Rio de Janeiro and San Francisco put together, with deep-sea freighters moored at every angle for miles in the roadstead, but to whose heroic prospect nearly the only human dwellings visible on this side of the water that had any air of belonging, or in which their inhabitants could be siad any longer to participate, were, paradoxically, a few lowly little self-built shacks and floathouses, that might have been driven out of the city altogether, down to the water's edge into the sea itself, where they stoon on piles, like fishermen's huts (which several of them apparently were), or on rollers, some dark and tumbledown, others freshly and prettily painted, these last quite evidently built or placed with some human need for beauty in mind, even if under the permanent threat of eviction, and all standing, even the most somber, with their fluted tin chimneys smoking here and there like toy tramp steamers, as though in defiance of the town, before eternity. In Enochvilleport itself some ghastly-colored neon signs had long since been going through their unctuous twitchings and gesticulations that nostalgia and love transform into a poetry of longing: more happily one began to flicker: *Palomar, Louis Armstrong and His Orchestra.* A huge new gray dead hotel that at sea might be a landmark of romance, belched smoke out of its turreted haunted-looking roof, as if it had caught fire, and beyond that all the lamps were blazing within the grim courtyard of the law courts, equally at sea a trysting place of the heart, outside which one of the stone lions, having recently been blown up, was covered reverently with a white cloth, and inside which for a month a group of stainless citizens had been trying a sixteen-year-old boy for murder.

Nearer the park the apron lights appeared on a sort of pebble-dashed Y.M.C.A.-Hall-cum-variety-theater saying *Tammuz The Master Hypnotist, To-nite 8:30,* and running past this the tramlines, down which another parkwise streetcar was approaching, could be seen extending almost to the department store in whose show window Tammuz' subject, perhaps a somnolent descendant of the seven sisters whose fame had eclipsed even that of the Pleiades, but whose announced ambition was to become a female psychiatrist, had been sleeping happily and publicly in a double bed for the last three days as an advance publicity stunt for tonight's performance.

Above Lost Lagoon on the road now mounting toward the suspension bridge in the distance much as a piece of jazz music mounts toward a break, a newsboy cried: "LASH ORDERED FOR SAINT PIERRE! SIXTEEN YEAR OLD BOY, CHILD –

SLAYER, TO HANG! Read all about it!''

The weather too was forboding. Yet, seeing the wandering lovers, the other passers-by on this side of the lagoon, a wounded soldier lying on a bench smoking a cigarette, and one or two of those destitute souls, the very old who haunt parks — since, faced with a choice, the very old will sometimes prefer, rather than to keep a room and starve, at least in such a city as this, somehow to eat and live outdoors — smiled too.

For as the girl walked along beside the man with her arm through his and as they smiled together and their eyes met with love, or they paused, watching the blowing seagulls, or the ever-changing scene of the snow-freaked Canadian mountains with their fleecy indigo chasms, or to listen to the deep-toungued majesty of a merchantman's echoing roar (these things that made Enochvilleport's ferocious aldermen imagine that it was the city itself that was beautiful, and maybe they were half right), the whistle of a ferryboat as it sidled across the inlet northward, what memories might not be evoked in a poor soldier, in the breasts of the bereaved, the old, even, who knows, in the mounted policemen, not merely of young love, but of lovers, as they seemed to be, so much in love that they were afraid to lose a moment of their time together?

Yet only a guardian angel of these two would have known — and surely they must have possessed a guardian angel — the strangest of all strange things of which they were thinking, save that, since they had spoken of it so often before, and especially, when they had opportunity, on this day of the year, each knew of course that the other was thinking about it, to such an extent indeed that it was no surprise, it only resembled the beginning of a ritual when the man said, as they entered the main path of the forest, through whose branches that shielded them from the wind could be made out, from time to time, suggesting a fragment of music manuscript, a bit of the suspension bridge itself:

''It was a day just like this that I set the boat adrift. It was twenty-nine years ago in June.''

"It was twenty-nine years ago in June, darling. And it was June twenty-seventh."

"It was five years before you were born, Astrid, and I was ten years old and I came down to the bay with my father."

"It was five years before I was born, you were ten years old, and you came down to the wharf with your father. Your father and grandfather had made you the boat between them and it was a fine one, ten inches long, smoothly varnished and made of wood from your model airplane box, with a new strong white sail."

"Yes, it was balsa wood from my model airplane box and my father sat beside me, telling me what to write for a note to put in it."

"Your father sat beside you, telling you what to write," Astrid laughed, "and you wrote:

"Hello.

"My name is Sigurd Storlesen. I am ten years old. Right now I am sitting on the wharf at Fearnought Bay, Clallam County, State of Washington, U.S.A., 5 miles south of Cape Flattery on the Pacific side, and my Dad is beside me telling me what to write. Today is June 27, 1922. My Dad is a forest warden in the Olympic National Forest but my Granddad is the lighthouse keeper at Cape Flattery. Beside me is a small shine canoe which you now hold in your hand. It is a windy day and my Dad said to put the canoe in the water when I have put this in and glued down the lid which is a piece of balsa wood from my model airplane box.

"Well must close this note now, but first I will ask you to tell the Seattle Star that you have found it, because I am going to start reading the paper from today and looking for a piece that says, who when and where it was found.

"Thanks. Sigurd Storlesen."

"Yes, then my father and I put the note inside, and we glued down the lid and sealed it and put the boat on the water."

"You put the boat on the water and the tide was going out and away it went. The current caught it right off and carried it out and you watched it till it was out of sight!''

The two had now reached a clearing in the forest where a few gray squirrels were scampering about on the grass. A dark-browed Indian in a windbreaker, utterly absorbed by his friendly task, stood with a sleek black squirrel sitting on his shoulder nibbling popcorn he was giving it from a bag. This reminded them to get some peanuts to feed the bears, whose cages were over the way.

Ursus Horribilis: and now they tossed peanuts to the sad lumbering sleep-heavy creatures — though at least these two grizzlies were together, they even had a home — maybe still too sleepy to know where they were, still wrapped in a dream of their timberfalls and wild blueberries in the Cordilleras Sigurd and Astrid could see again, straight ahead of them, between the trees, beyond a bay.

But how should they stop thinking of the little boat?

Twelve years it had wandered. Through the tempests of winter, over sunny summer seas, what tide rips had caught it, what wild sea birds, shearwaters, storm petrels, jaegers, that follow the thrashing propellers, the dark albatross of these northern waters, swooped upon it, or warm currents edged it lazily toward land — and blue-water currents sailed it after the albacore, with fishing boats like white giraffes — or glacial drifts tossed it about fuming Cape Flattery itself. Perhaps it had rested, floating in a sheltered cove, where the killer whale smote, lashed, the deep clear water; the eagle and the salmon had seen it, a baby seal stared with her wondering eyes, only for the little boat to be thrown aground, catching the rainy afternoon sun, on cruel barnacled rocks by the waves, lying aground knocked from side to side in an inch of water like a live thing, or a poor old tin can, pushed, pounded ashore, and swung around, reversed again, left high and dry, and then swept another yard up the beach, or carried under a lonely salt-gray shack, to drive a seine fisherman crazy all night with its faint plaintive knocking, before it ebbed out in the dark autumn dawn, and found its way afresh, over the deep, coming through thunder, to who will ever know what fierce and desolate uninhabited shore, known only to the dread Wendigo, where not even an Indian could have found it, unfriended there, lost, until it was borne out to sea once more by the great brimming black tides of January, or the huge calm tides of the midsummer moon, to start its journey all over again ——

Astrid and Sigurd came to a large enclosure, set back from a walk, with two vine-leaved maple trees (their scarlet tassels, delicate precursors of their leaves, already visible) growing through the top, a sheltered cavernous part to one side for a a lair, and the whole, save for the barred front, covered with stout large-meshed wire — considered sufficient protection for one of the most Satanic beasts left living on earth.

Two animals inhabited the cage, spotted like deceitful pastel leopards, and in appearance like decorated, maniacal-looking cats: their ears were provided with huge tassels and, as if this were in savage parody of the vine-leaved maples, from the brute's chin tassels also depended. Their legs were as long as a man's arm, and their paws, clothed in gray fur out of which shot claws curved like scimitars, were as big as a man's clenched fist.

And the two beautiful demonic creatures prowled and paced endlessly, searching the base of their cage, between whose bars there was just room to slip a murderous paw — always a hop out of reach an invisible sparrow went pecking away in the dust — searching with eternal voraciousness, yet seeking in desperation also some way out, passing and repassing each other rhythmically, as though truly damned and under some compelling enchantment.

And yet as they watched the terrifying Canadian lynx, in which seemed to be embodied in animal form all the pure ferocity of nature, as they watched, crunching peanuts themselves now and passing the bag between them, before the lovers' eyes still sailed that tiny boat, battling with the seas, at the mercy of a wilder ferocity yet, all those years before Astrid was born.

Ah, its absolute loneliness amid those wastes, those wildernesses of rough rainy seas bereft even of sea birds, between contrary winds, or in the great dead windless swell that comes following a gale; and then with the wind springing up and blowing the spray across the sea like rain, like a vision of creation, blowing the little boat as it climbed the highlands into the skies, from which sizzled cobalt lightenings, and then sank down into the abyss, but already was climbing again, while the whole sea crested with foam like lambs' wool went furling off to leeward, the whole vast moon-driven expanse like the pastures and valleys and snow-capped ranges of a Sierra Madre in delirium, in ceaseless motion, rising and falling, and the little boat rising, and falling into a paralyzing sea of white drifting fire and smoking spume by which it seemed overwhelmed: and all this time a sound, like a high sound of singing, yet as sustained in harmony as telegraph wires, or like the unbelievably high perpetual sound of the wind where there is nobody to listen, which perhaps does not exist, or the ghost of the wind in the rigging of ships long lost, and perhaps it was the sound of the wind in its toy rigging, as again the boat slanted onward: but even then what further unfathomed deeps had it oversailed, until what birds of ill omen turned heavenly for it at last, what iron birds with saber wings skimming forever through the murk above the gray immeasurable swells, imparted mysteriously their own homing knowledge to it: the lonely buoyant little craft, nudging it with their beaks under golden sunsets in a blue sky, as it sailed close in to mountainous coasts of clouds with stars over them, or burning coasts at sunset once more, as it rounded not only the terrible spume-drenched rocks, like incinerators in sawmills, of Flattery, but other capes unknown, those twelve years, of giant pinnacles, images of barrenness and desolation, upon which the heart is thrown and impaled eternally! — And strangest of all now many ships themselves had threatened it, during that voyage of only some three score miles as the crow flies from its launching to its final port, looming out of the fog and passing by harmlessly all those years — those years too of the last sailing ships, rigged to the moonsail, sweeping by into their own oblivion — but ships cargoed with guns or iron for impending wars, what freighters now at the bottom of the sea he, Sigurd, had voyaged in for that matter, freighted with old marble and wine and cherries-in-brine, or whose engines even now were still somewhere murmuring: *Frere* Jacques! *Frere* Jacques!

What strange poem of God's mercy was this?

Suddenly across their vision a squirrel ran up a tree beside the cage and then, chattering shrilly, leaped from a branch and darted across the top of the wire mesh. Instantly, swift and deadly as lightning, one of the lynx sprang twenty feet into the air, hurtling straight to the top of the cage toward the squirrel, hitting the wire with a twang like a mammoth guitar, and simultaneously flashing through the wire its scimitar claws: Astrid cried out and covered her face.

But the squirrel, unhurt, untouched, was already running lightly along another branch, down to the tree, and away, while the infuriated lynx sprang straight up, sprang again, and again and again and again, as his mate crouched spitting and snarling below.

Sigurd and Astrid began to laugh. Then this seemed obscurely unfair to the lynx, now solemnly washing his mate's face. The innocent squirrel, for whom they felt such relief, might almost have been showing off, almost, unlike the oblivious sparrow, have been taunting the caged animal. The squirrel's hairbreadth escape — the thousand-to-one chance — that on second thought must take place every day, seemed meaningless. But all at once it did not seem meaningless that they had been there to see it.

"You know how I watched the paper and waited," Sigurd was saying, stopping to relight his pipe, as they walked on.

"The Seattle *Star*," Astrid said.

"The Seattle *Star* . . . It was the first newspaper I ever read. Father always declared the boat had gone south — maybe to Mexico, and I seem to remember Granddad saying no, if it didn't break up on Tatoosh, the tide would take it right down Juan de Fuca Strait, maybe into Puget Sound itself. Well, I watched and waited for a long time and finally, as kids will, I stopped looking."

"And the years went on —"

"And I grew up. Granddad was dead by then. And the old man, you know about him. Well, he's dead too now. But I never forgot. Twelve years! Think of it —! Why, it voyaged around longer than we've been married."

"And we've been married seven years."

"Seven years today —"

"It seems like a miracle!"

But their words fell like spent arrows before the target of this fact.

They were walking, as they left the forest, between two long rows of Japanese cherry trees, next month to be an airy avenue of celestial bloom. The cherry trees behind, the forest reappeared, to left and right of the wide clearing, and skirting two arms of the bay. As they approached the Pacific, down the gradual incline, on this side remote from the harbor the wind grew more boisterous: gulls, glaucous and raucous, wheeled and sailed overhead, yelling, and were suddenly far out to sea.

And it was the sea that lay before them, at the end of the slope that changed into the steep beach, the naked sea, running deeply below, without embankment or promenade, or any friendly shacks, though some prettily built homes showed to the left, with one light in a window, glowing warmly through the trees on the edge of the forest itself, as of some stalwart Columbian Adam, who had calmly stolen back with his Eve into Paradise, under the flaming sword of the civic cherubim.

The tide was low. Offshore, white horses were running around a point. The headlong onrush of the tide of beaten silver flashing over its crossflowing underset was so fast the very surface of the sea seemed racing away.

Their path gave place to a cinder track in the familiar lee of an old frame pavilion, a deserted tea house boarded up since last summer. Dead leaves were slithering across the porch, past which on the slope to the right picnic benches, tables, a derelict swing, lay overturned, under a tempestuous grove of birches. It seemed cold, sad, inhuman there, and beyond,with the roar of that deep low tide. Yet there was that between the lovers which moved like a warmth, and might have thrown open the shutters, set the benches and tables aright, and filled the whole grove with the voices and children's laughter of summer. Astrid paused for a moment with a hand on Sigurd's arm while they were sheltered by the pavilion, and said, what she too had often said before, so that they always repeated these things almost like an incantation:

"I'll never forget it. That day when I was seven years old, coming to the park here on a picnic with my father and mother and brother. After lunch my brother and I came down to the beach to play. It was a fine summer day, and the tide was out, but there'd been this very high tide in the night, and you could see the lines of driftwood and seaweed where it had ebbed. . . . was playing on the beach, and I found your boat.!"

"You were playing on the beach and you found my boat. And the mast was broken."

"The mast was broken and shreds of sail hung dirty and limp. But your boat was still whole and unhurt, though it was scratched and weatherbeaten and the varnish was gone. I ran to my mother, and she saw the sealing wax over the cockpit, and, darling, I found your note.

"You found our note, my darling."

Astrid drew from her pocket a scrap of paper and holding it between them they bent over (though it was hardly legible by now and they knew it off by heart) and read:

> Hello.
>
> My name is Sigurd Storlesen. I am ten years old. Right now I am sitting on the wharf at Fearnought Bay, Clallam County, State of Washington, U.S.A., 5 miles south of Cape Flattery on the Pacific side, and my Dad is beside me telling me what to

write. Today is June 27, 1922. My Dad is a forest warden in the Olympic National Forest but my Granddad is the lighthouse keeper at Cape Flattery. Beside me is a small shiny canoe which you now hold in your hand. It is a windy day and my Dad said to put the canoe in the water when I have put this in and glued down the lid which is a piece of balsa wood from my model airplane box.

Well must close this note now, but first I will ask you to tell the Seattle Star that you have found it, because I am going to start reading the paper from today and looking for a piece that says, who when and where it was found.

Thanks.

Sigurd Storlesen.

They came to the desolate beach strewn with driftwood, sculptured, whorled, silvered, piled everywhere by tides so immense there was a tideline of seaweed and detritus on the grass behind them, and great logs and shingle-bolts and writhing snags, curcificial, or frozen in a fiery rage — or better, a few bits of lumber almost ready to burn, for someone to take home, and automatically they threw them up beyond the sea's reach for some passing soul, remembering their own winters of need — and more snags there at the foot of the grove and visible high on the sea-scythed forest banks on either side, in which riven trees were growing, yearning over the shore. And everywhere they looked was wreckage, the toll of winter's wrath: wrecked hencoops, wrecked floats, the wrecked side of a fisherman's hut, its boards once hammered together, with its wrenched shiplap and extruding nails. The fury had extended even to the beach itself, formed in hummocks and waves and barriers of shingle and shells they had to climb up in places. And everywhere too was the grotesque macabre fruit of the sea, with its exhilarating iodine smell, nightmarish bulbs of kelp like antiquated motor horns, trailing brown satin streamers twenty feet long, sea wrack like demons, or the discarded casements of evil spirits that had been cleansed. Then more wreckage: boots, a clock, torn fishing nets, a demolished wheelhouse, a smashed wheel lying in the sand.

Nor was it possible to grasp for more than a moment that all this with its feeling of death and destruction and barrenness was only an appearance, that beneath the flotsam, under the very shells they crunched, within the trickling overflows of winterbournes they jumped over, down at the tide margin, existed, just as in the forest, a stirring and stretching of life, a seething of spring.

When Astrid and Sigurd were almost sheltered by an uprooted tree on one of these lower billows of beach they noticed that the clouds had lifted over the sea, though the sky was not blue but still that intense silver, so that they could see right across the Gulf and make out, or thought they could, the line of some Gulf Islands. A lone freighter with upraised derricks shipped seas on the horizon. A hint of the summit of Mount Hood remained, or it might have been clouds. They remarked too, in the southeast, on the sloping base of a hill, a triangle of storm-washed green, as if cut out of the overhanging murk there, in which were four pines, five telegraph posts, and a clearing resembling a cemetery. Behind them the icy mountains of Canada hid their savage peaks and snowfalls under still more savage clouds. And they saw that the sea was gray with white-caps and currents charging offshore and spray blowing backwards from the rocks.

But when the full force of the wind caught them, looking from the shore, it was like gazing into chaos. The wind blew away their thoughts, their voices, almost their very senses, as they walked, crunching the shells, laughing and stumbling. Nor could they tell whether it was spume or rain that smote and stung their faces, whether spindrift from the sea or rain from which the sea was born, as now finally they were forced to a halt, standing there arm in arm. . . . And it was to this shore, through that chaos, by those currents, that their little boat with its innocent message had been brought out of the past finally to safety and a home.

But ah, the storms they had come through!

GEORGE BOWERING was born fifty years ago in the Okanagan Valley of B.C. and has subsequently produced some forty volumes of fiction or poetry. Educated at U.B.C. he has received a Governor General's Award for his poetry in 1969 and another for fiction in 1980 for his *Burning Water*. He resides in Vancouver and teaches at Simon Fraser University.

GEORGE BOWERING

Ebbe & Hattie

Sometimes I think I'm just a chorus, for Christ sake, there's a gigantic drama or maybe comedy going on, the hero is Ebbe, he is travailing thru act two scene three & after a violent or outrageous scene, there I am, popping up & singing a few verses, offering my myopic commentary that straightens it all out, the story summarized, the men in bluejeans moving the sets around & when I fade away among the cardboard boulders the lights man is ready to illuminate the stage for the next act, maybe the sub-plot. On the other hand, poets get fixations & call them themes, mistaken critters all.

You are already aware of the difficulty I'm having. I'm not clear about the relationship between Ebbe & myself. I'm now old enough to admit to myself that I love him, his lovely shape & romantic head & the white soul that's been under the ground too long, away from the sun, even the soft Vancouver sun, old friend. He makes me edgy too, because he has some immediacy about him, his judgement, he knows when I sidestep toward phoniness before I do & I resent it, & I almost worship it. He makes me —

He makes me impatient at times, but also respectful. If he was a mortician & I was his wife, that's how I would feel, when his hands toucht my body after his day's work. A kind of respect, too.

Or, finally, put it this way: I am the English, transporting the marble artwork from the Parthenon to this Victoria & Albert Museum to make it safe from destruction on its Greek hill. Ebbe is the Turkish Air Force, bombing the hell out of the ancient building in their total campaign against Athens. Who's the more artistic? I ask you.

Artistic. Yep, those of you who've known me for a little while. Delsing, ah Christ, will know that I am no shrinking daffodil when it comes to what my grey brain thinks of itself — though I say brain, I mean like you say, mind. That is, what I'm trying to say, so badly again, is that it really has taken some movement of hidden DNA material to have me admit first to myself & then to all of you, that I felt I was learning something from Ebbe, younger Ebbe, bare ass bouncing up & down, that I didn't know before, even in the early years. God knows, from his silence now in that place in the middle of my childhood valley, what he could teach me now. What the heck is he, younger brother with all the things left out of me, the older one; or guru, as is the fashion to say these days, further along in the sixties. Maybe both.

You can tell, I suppose, that I'm putting off telling something. I am. Mainly because it's from an incident that shows Ebbe in a light that doesn't shine anymore, but maybe that's okay too, because maybe you can understand something from the following incident that I don't understand at all. Take a chance, take a chance, Delsing, okay. That's one of the things he clarified for me, that lover.

The cast of characters grows.The scene is an early summer day in the early sixties, say 61, I have borrowed my roomy Bob Small's yellow Morris Minor with the broken radio, & Ebbe & I are on our way to Kerrisdale. Kerrisdale — it's a once-fashionable residential section up the hill & south of downtown, full of venerable trees, this is before they started erecting all the pink apartment cells with balconies, it's all houses with big lawns covered with tricycles, stucco houses, with glass front doors, glass doorknobs, cracks in the sidewalks, gleam off the glass in the brown stucco on the front wall, our prof's house.

He's a good prof, the only man I know who knows how to write about new poetry and all, but I'm not going to tell you his name because you'll just go looking for him. But for those who could profit (no, not with money) I'll give you a hint — he's from a little town in Washington. So in we go, me first in my usual gangbusters way, grabbing his wife & kissing her forehead where there's a bit of sweaty hair, she's been bending over an oven, so I grab a bunch of her brand new peanut-butter cookies, & I flop in the six-foot couch in the living room, look through the new records scattered on the floor & coffee tables. Ebbe comes in slower, cooler, remember he's Miles Davis, I'm Cannonball Adderly, or Cornball Latterly, & a chattery lover at that. Ebbe says hi very softly, & is in his pre-argument or pre-shouting mood. Prof likes us both in our various ways, & he has some Bourbon, which is unusual around Vancouver livingrooms, & we quaff away, me wondering what branch water is.

"So, what have you been up to?" Asks Prof.

"Writing short but passionate lyrics," Says I.

"Listening to music along the train tracks," says Ebbe, or something like that. I half listen & half compose, & that's what you're getting now, literature.

Oh um ah, we talk along, & it aint really working very well, & I think ah Ebbe what's going thru your oblangata now, old murky Arabian plains & unfinisht poems crust to rubble under the pee of your pet pup. So I suggested that we're going to Stanley Park & environs, & we'll take the kids. The kids are boy & girl, she's pretty as her mom, ten years old, & he's a shave-head, seven, & away we go, bourbon sloshing in our bouncing bellies, or mine anyway.

Kerrisdale westward — the drive takes you to either the Indian reserve where I aint been, or Marine Drive, the twisty road that looks like a country road except there aint any hills, you go between the tall trees someone has left on the edge of the city, spruces, swooping & zanging around the bends, made more dangerous because Ebbe & I have a half-gallon of loganberry wine, & we're glugging it as he drives, & to begin with Ebbe aint much of a driver, never having lived in the mountains except when he was a little kid, & some racial memory driving, hurtling him along. We're giving some of the juice to Barry & Bonny too, & they love it, it tastes so grownup & a little sweet, good old berry cup for $1.55 a half gallon, & some of it glows red on all our shirtfronts. We drove along the snaky road toward Spanish Banks, which I have explained many times, the eroding cliffs where the sailors from Acapulco used to hang out before Cap Vancouver made his approach and subsequent deal. Along the way we passt the tea house where me & Marce have gone for lunchtime pot of tea & muffins, attended all alone in the big old room by the lady in the apron, & we see where the old road used to go west of it, but that's fallen into the sea now, & the pavement just goes away into the air over Wreck Beach, the loving place where there is a legendary gold-filled boat of sails out there under the log booms on the glistening water.

This road, you might as well know, eventually passes the university on the hill that I've attended for some time as trench-coat bard of the coffee table, much to the disgust of many truer hearts, & we're taking it for its lovely swerves (at 50 miles an hour, oh me) & the fact that it goes right by the women's dorm, where friendly Hattie lives.

Hattie is a girl I've never mentioned before because I love her soul. She has a thing she does, which is prerequisite for living in Vancouver, but I love her mainly for the way she deciphers me & the deeper country things I'm feeling. Hattie is the centre of us & whatever love we may have found for each other, & like any hub she's round, round bum & round boobies & round head, ah, even her cheeks round, so the first thing I wanted to do was pinch her cheeks & the second was to lie on the bare belly, which I've done in the times I needed a face close to mine & keeping all eyes open. Hattie is the real artist among all us artists in the nerve warfare, she's calm & makes brown & green pots from the earth, tapestries, candles, every one of us wears a shirt Hattie made. I don't know how many of us have gone up to the Cariboo country & rested on a couch covered with doeskin & on the large wild lawn in the front of her father's ranch house. I mean ranch house, not ranch-style house. I mean that about Hattie too. I went up there once, beautiful air, eating the small strawberries that grow on the ground that grades from lawn to rolling brown hills. She didn't let us speak our lies & boasts & self-proclamations without feeling some foolishness, & that's where she had us, fools. A beautiful girl, Hattie, woman, same age as me, with her big teeth & chubby legs & wild brown hair that I used to arrange on her shoulders on that couch in the Cariboo.

She lived in the women's dorm in a sense, that is she had a name on the door there, & she didn't sneak out in the time when she was supposed to have a pass, she just went & came, & they didn't do anything about it, to like, punish her. I guess that tells more about her than I've been trying to.

She used to say to me, "George, it's just an act, the way you mope & sulk around the city in your sneakers & Rimbaud moods. The nice thing about you is when I see that you're still a back country boy with polka dot hankie."

Yeah, well, there's no need my explaining Hattie too much, except it's noteworthy that she is my age, about four years or so older than Ebbe, I suppose, though most of the time that doesn't make any difference, I mean to anybody.

Ebbe sat there revving the motor & passing the berry jug with the kids while I went in to get her, stopping at the desk in the lobby where the lady with the iron hair sat at her desk, & I rang Hat up on the phone & down she came in less than a minute, wearing a blouse & skirt & stockings with runs in them, her hair clutcht together with an elastic band. I gave her a hug at the door of the elevator, & walkt outside with my arm around her shoulder. She had paint in the edges of her fingernails.

"Into the car with yuh," I said, & Ebbe took off in third gear, humping & snorting down the road. Most of the way I couldn't see because the big bottle, half empty now, was between me & the windshield.

"What's out there? Where are we?" I shouted.

"Never mind, it's all inscape, inscape," said Ebbe, & then "Glub."

"Let George drive," yelled Barry.

"Please!" added Bonny.

"No whining!" hollered Ebbe, shifting from fourth into low for the hill below the arts building, & we swoopt down more, me spilling wine on Hattie's blouse every time Ebbe shifted gears in his frantic efforts to find the right one.

"Oh, man, that tastes good," said Bonny.

"Come on, Ebbe, let George drive," said Barry.

I turned around & smiled at Hattie in the back seat with the kids. "Aint Ebbe great, though?" I askt. "Fangio of the yellow Morris Miracle, zanging at forty-five along Marine Drive, past the lugubrious gulls of the Jericho Hill tennis court."

"Aint never been in court in my life," said Ebbe, & I knew it was getting to him. Ebbe never said things like that when he was stoned, & I'd never seen him drunk on BC wine. Ah, but I had my image to uphold.

"Calabash!" I hollered, my head out the window.

Hattie wasn't laughing. She wasn't out of it, but she was just about the calmest girl I ever met. The first time I ever went to bed with her she knew it was because of the perplexities of my love life, & it was four in the morning, but she just opened the covers & let me in to lie on her warm belly. Ah. I turned & smiled at her & told her I love her. I guess you do, she said from the back seat of the car.

The kids were drunk as hell when we got to Stanley Park. They shouted & demanded wine & chased one another among the big ferns under the trees. This was before I'd ever seen the park from on top of a peyote button, & it was just big trees, lovely dark & deep. We walkt, the jug dangling from Ebbe's hand, & I did my usual thing, going out in front & seeing everything first. Ebbe disappeared for a minute & came back without the bottle, & I knew maybe I was seeing everything first but he was seeing everything best. Ah, I'll never beat him. & I don't care, now. He's behind his Valley cabin, watching the fish coming to feed at the top of the stream.

"Hattie, Hattie, Hattie, Hattie," he said, walking under a low branch so that a twig broke off & snagged in his thick black hair.

"Hpfhh, you wood sprite," she said, the sun bright on her wide forehead.

We came out of the trees on a parking & viewing place overlooking the reach of storied Lions Gate Bridge, & there were a couple bright red phone booths. I gave Barry his orders & dropt in a dime & called Prof's number. When he came on, there was little loaded Barry saying

"No thcruples, paw."

Ebbe enjoyed that, & I was thinking well I is getting thru to him, & just then the sun came thru brighter than ever, on Hattie's forehead, on the blonde hair of the kids, across the wavy expanse of Burrard Inlet. Ebbe was standing under a tree, & the bright sun made deep black shadows on him. He was writing in his notebook. He always wrote poems a lot different from ours, the rest of us. He said the source of the act was the darkness. He stood in it. Hattie gave the sense of understanding. I was baffled a little, & a little scornful. I said write about what you see. Ebbe said that what you see may be alright, but it might be what somebody wants you to see.

Like my love poems. Like my love.

We fell by the parking lot on the way to the animals, & sat in the car & glugged some more of the juice, all in order, Barry last. He smelled like Powell Street already, old berry cup all over him, little kid in his cups.

"This is awful, getting a defenseless kid slosht," said Ebbe.

"No thcruples, paw," said Barry.

(I'm telling about this day because it's the kind of day we used to have there on the coast, no thundering drama, no suicide, no murder, just a walk in the park.)

& pretty soon, we're taking it in &/or making notes. I mean Ebbe had his endless brown notepad out & was writing in it with his old-fashioned italic script fountain pen of black ink & beautiful Chinese calligraphic English or German, & at the best of times it would be like the illuminated texts of yore, but now I wondered, because Ebbe was staggering somewhat thru the forest till Bonny said "If Ebbe drives on the way home I'm going to walk," but Ebbe didn't hear, just kept on saying oh yeah, the trees, & of course the rest of us took to wandering in our own ways, taking notes as I told myself I was doing inside my own romantic brain, knowing that all the time Hattie was really into it, just finding her joyous way despite our stasis among the trees. She has a broad & slightly flat face, Eskimo face I always thought then, & if she stood still in the forest where no one was around to make noises the inch worms hanging from their threads on the trees would land on her shoulder & curl up in sensuous relaxation. But not on Ebbe, his frog legs springing him around from side to side as he noted the hexagons of springtime Pacific cloudlight on the forefex of a tree or something. At least that's what I either suspected at the time or recast now in this blacksmith brain (see Ben Jonson).

Nothing is happening, right? Oh, you're so wrong. Or maybe I'm underestimating you. Well, that's really underestimating myself as badly.

We came finally to a kind of symbol. This is Lumberman's Arch. It's a landmark in Vancouver, integrated into the normal walks of people's Sundays now, but at the time just getting free from the newspaper photograph focus it was getting, as a symbol, I say. Lumberman's Arch is not really an arch in the classic sense, it's more a westcoast structure, made as it is from that content, three chunks of spruce tree, two vertical & one stretching across on an incline, over the smooth road that wanders thru the eastern part of the park where people take their kids to ride on the ponies at the children's zoo, near the breakwater in view of the Lions Gate Bridge. (Oh, did we ever make water at the breakwater.) Not only content though —more importantly, form, as they say, the other aspect of the presentation of an — art form. Well, it's a very conscious thing, lets's say that, & it really isn't as large as it may be rumored to be by tourists who take pictures of their wives standing against it with the North Shore mountains of snowcap in the background.

Remembering it now, I can't remember now we got to the top of it, first Ebbe, & then myself. I followed him up there because I could hear the kids worrying about him in his drunken state on the high incline, walking from the lower end to the higher, on the tube of wood, one foot in front of the other, walking upright with a notebook & fountain pen in his hands, not looking at the road below or the inland sea in front of his face. I lookt at Hattie & she didn't say anything, but I saw her beginning to say something with her large grey eyes, & so I climbed up, how I don't know or remember, & followed him, on my feet, but with my hands touching the wood, like a monkey free from the cages to my right up the grassy hill, or like a man beginning a trackmeet dash, waiting for the starter's gun or my head crasht against the pavement below.

He was up at the high end now. He was sitting down, a skinny leg in black denim hanging over each side, his pen at the notebook. Jesus, how well do I know this kid, I askt myself. So I lookt over his shoulder & he was writing a lot of black ink sloppy italic writing, & what I could read went:

> Oh Hattie of the Horse's flowers, Hattie,
> skull like a loving cup
> Hattie, suet belly Hattie, hot honey nest
> Hattie, I'm so drunk take me to a stationary
> room Hattie ——

etc etc etc. I tapt him on the shoulder & said, "Any time you want to come down, oh mighty tree-topper." & I turned around carefully & millimetered my way to the ground again, where the kids grabbed me & made their various pleas.

I held Hattie's arm and walkt with her over to where the small deer were standing with their bums toward some kids who were throwing potato chips over the low fence. The potato chips caught in the air & floated in every direction. The pigeons pounced them to bits with their hard noses. One of the pigeons hopt around on one foot, the other nowhere in sight. He was the fattest of them all.

''Ebbe's funny today,'' said Hattie.

''Isn't he funny all the time?'' I askt. Brilliant words. I was inspired by the ghost of Pauline Johnson in the trees.

I'd love to take Hattie into the trees. Once we were parkt in the car in front of the women's dorm & I had my hand on her warmth, & she was straining forward in the seat, & eventually I came hotly in my pants, it was so sudden. That hadn't happened for years, not since the days of you know who back in Lawrence. Another time, & during the time of another girl, I went to Hattie for comfort & she said is she doing that much to you, & I lay on her mattress on the floor with her long small-town hair lying on the tenders skin of my belly. I know Hattie was at that time a comfort to all of us, & the nicest Sunday afternoon I ever spent was the time I sat naked in the sunshine of my window while she fed cool potter's clay to her long fingers, fashioning an image of my body.

Now I could have put my hand on the cotton over one of her big breasts, but I lifted her long hair & kisst the back of her neck.

''Hattie, I love you.''

''I know,'' she said, & pointed at the deer. One was licking the other's face.

Bonny & Barry were yelling somewhere behind us. We both turned instinctively toward Lumberman's Arch. There was Ebbe standing on it with his hands together over his head, streamlined position for a spectacular swan dive. Below him was a cop on a horse. I was glad the wine bottle was in the bushes near the car. I walkt up & stood near the cop, just out of range of a club.

''That there's my friend Ebbe,'' I said.

''Well, you tell your friend to come down or I'll bash his bloody head in,'' said the cop. The horse stood very still.

The cop had an English accent. A few years earlier that would have made me argumentative. Hattie cleared her throat behind me.

"'Go screw your poodle!'' he hollered, retiring from gleamy dive to mere arm-waving, feet curling on the round British Columbia log. The cop fidgeted on his horse, leather creaking.

''Ebbe — '' said Hattie, & that did it as I never could have. Ebbe started walking down the slope & lookt like he was going to make it, me following him on the ground, the horse shivering flies off his buttocks. Bonny & Barry hopping up & down with consternation on their professor's children's foreheads, but Barry burying a big wine burp in his anxiety. & then Ebbe came tumbling down (as he always has been ever since), heel kicking bark loose, but there I was just below him, & I placed my heroic body before his fall. Satan or protector I don't know, but arms out as if I'm going to catch a high fly ball, & he hits me with a spindly whump, & we both go down. We are in one another's arms, rolling, & Ebbe gives me a big kiss.

''No thcruples,'' he says. & his delicate black hair head is down there surrounded by horse hoofs, & I'm thinking as I roll out of the way that my friend is going to die a newspaper poet death but his head lies there, his face looking straight up & no arms in front of his eyes, the horse's steel feet banging the pavement beside his ears, oh what confusion.

Oh please don't send us to jail says Hattie in her way, & for some reason we got out of it, maybe the cop was scared by almost killing Eb, just as years later there's a love-in a few hundred yards from here, a thousand people in weird clothes & flowers circulating around Country Joe & the Fish, the best rock band in the world, & there's Ebbe in a shirt made by his wife, yellow flowers in his thick hair, walking around (& there's Bonny too, by the way, a teenager now with braces on her teeth & a long white gown, stoned to the ears & later in the newspaper photos) & up on the hill nearby is a Stanley Park cop on a still horse like the Indian in the painting, & a newspaper guy goes up to him & says what are those people smoking, & the cop points at Ebbe & says ask him.

Yep, thank God, he let us go, & I didn't wind up in the Vancouver jail till a few years later, but this time we watcht the ass of the cop's horse waddling by the sea wall, & we walkt the other way, to get popcorn to soak up the red wine in the kids bellies, which they liked, the sweet children, & I followed Ebbe thru lugubrious halls of the dark clammy aquarium where he fell on his knees in front of the giant sea turtles —

"I aint *got* a poodle, even," I said after we got out in the soft-air Vancouver sunshine.

"Figure of speech, you dumb prose-writer."

"Ah, bargel dargle, the waves of the inland sea between your ears," I countered.

This time I drove Small's car, & the kids were a little happier & so was I, & in the back seat Ebbe laid his head on Hattie's ample lap — the west coast & wine in the afternoon make all the young men sleepy — & I drove with one eye on the rear-view mirror, following the sparks of a Number 7 bus up the hill of Dunbar, remembering that years ago in Lawrence me & Small fell in love with a lifeguard lady said she lived on Dunbar & every time I drove there I wondered where she was now, probably sending her oldest daughter off to the nearby school of another sorrow.

"Where we going?" askt Barry.

"Taking you home, little wino," I said, & we zanged east on 41st Avenue, Ebbe's head an angel on Hattie's country mound.

We turned off the main drag into the street of tall trees where Prof lived, a little scrupulous, but lo & befuddle, the kids walkt straight in, already understanding no mention of the wine, & there was nothing at all, nothing at all, to worry about. Have a beer, we were askt, excluding the kids, & we did, & lookt at some of the new poetry magazines, & took off our shoes on the new soft rug, & spoke of the creative writing department at the university on the hill, & thought nothing of the future when all our friends would die, & it was the usual friendly scene at Prof's house, & I thought some day I'll dedicate a book to this house, & at that time I didn't know the half of it, of the time for instance when I would walk into the room to see my number one & final girl sitting on the couch touching belly buttons with Irwin Garden, the most famous poet of his generation, ah, but that is all to come in later stories maybe. At this moment there were whispering & smiles between Hattie & Ebbe, & off we went again, this time farther east to the place Bob Small & I rented on the third floor of the wood building on the steep slope overfalling False Creek mouth, legends legends all over the place — the Indians still run the northwest coast, remember & Klahowya, Tillicums.

(That last bit for oldtime childhood readers of the Vancouver *Province,* 1945.)

It was dark when we got there, we needed supper, beans & eggs & cold riceballs from the icebox, Small was there, & already in his pyjamas, studying like a bastard as he always did, so serious. Munch munch, the cold rice on top of old sloshing Calona or New Westminster red wine, & you can tell I want to get onto something else.

& this is it. One of the scenes I will always have in that personal past, not much to do with the way the westcoast was, & I want to record it (as you've guesst), but an important image of Ebbe, & that's what this is all about. I'll never forget it, or understand it. Or more important than that, I have finally realized after all the years — how I feel myself.

It was dark except for the brass gooseneck desk lamp beside me (& it's the one beside me as I tell you this), & I was sitting there on a stool with my looseleaf of poems on my knee & reading them because I suggested that & was welcomed. I was reading, & not taking my eyes off the light on the white paper in front of me.

On his bed between me & them was Bob Small, my boyhood chum who told me about his first jackoff those years long ago. He was sitting in a lazy lotus position & intently watching.

There on the other side of him was my bed, & Ebbe was holding up the blanket behind which Hattie was taking her clothes off or enough of them anyway, the sheet slipping & I saw Ebbe's long thin crooked cock for a moment & went back to my page. Then they met under the blanket, & I had never been so close to anyone else making love before, the boy who this afternoon kisst me, & the girl who first had my bud in her warm round mouth, & I felt like the perfect friend, reading my poems in praise of the lonely life in Vancouver's streets & on the slick wharves of railroad tracks. Small watcht as I listened & what I heard was my voice with the poems, the soft cries of Hattie & the heavy breath of little Ebbe, & the horse's hoofs pounding around my head.

BETTY LAMBERT was born in Calgary in 1933 and died prematurely in her fiftieth year. Her significant contributions to Canadian letters included several radio plays broadcast by the C.B.C., an hilarious comedy *Scrieux De Dieu,* and, above all, her searingly honest novel *Crossings* from which we offer an excerpt.

BETTY LAMBERT

an excerpt from the novel

Crossings

We had landed in Vancouver with eighty-eight dollars. We found a room in a West Georgia rooming house for eleven dollars a week. Hot plate. You washed your dishes in the bathtub. Or I did. I suppose other people carried basins back to their rooms. I counted the people who used the bathroom once. Twenty-eight. In the basement there were drug pushers. The Mounties broke down the door one night. It was all very exciting. I was sure I'd heard a shot, but perhaps it was wishful thinking. On the second floor the two prostitutes lived. And Erica and Karl, six weeks out from Germany. Across from us on the third floor lived the Cinderella Man. That's what he called himself. Grey suits, old school ties — all the old schools, with an entree into any world you could imagine. Was I interested in becoming a journalist? He personally would speak to the editor of the Sun. Actually, don't tell anyone, but he was living here incognito, doing research on the drug scene for a series of articles. Did Karl want to be a bartender? Fifty dollars to sweeten the union steward. The Cinderella Man could fix anything. To our left, the son of a man who'd been murdered. A famous case. He showed us the book about it. His father had designed the Empress Hotel. I felt I was really living at last. This was life.

Six months later I took half a bottle of 222's. Ben watched me, refusing to interfere. After all, it was my life. It was my decision. Made of my own free will. After I passed out, he took what was

No. He took a few of what was left. There were still some in the bottle the next morning.

No. We were not drunk. I had fallen in love. Tra la. But of course I was not unfaithful. I? I could not love thee, dear, so much, loved I not Honour more.

And I got asthma.

While I was in the hospital, Ben got a job, and that job turned into another job, and it was permanent. I got better and went to university. We stay married. There are always a lot of people around and they all say we are so lucky. No, what they actually say is, I am so lucky to have a husband like Ben.

* * * * *

It's a year later, almost a year. Yes, a year. I am divorced now. I'm in West Vancouver doing housework for a week and Jocelyn phones.

"We rented the room!"

"Oh good."

"To a man."

"Yeah, well, we knew that might happen."

"Well, I figure we can use the money."

"What's he like?"

"He's a clerk at city hall."

I see a pale blonde man, glasses, concave chest.

"That sounds all right."

"So when you coming home?"

Mik tells me his side of the story later.

He'd been out of the Pen about eight months. Living downtown on Granville Street, in hotels that have names like The Helen's and The Queen's. He was sitting in The Helen's one day and he decided to go across the bridge. To sit in The Helen's is distinct from to crash at The Helen's. If you sit, you are in the beer parlor. *To go across the bridge* means to go straight, become respectable, get a job. He was just sitting there, boozing it up with the buddies, and it came over him, how he had to go across the bridge. When he got out of the Pen he was still gimpy but Welfare fixed his back and then he did the odd bit of benny snatching and so on to augment his Welfare cheques. A bit of B & E now and then. Most times he crashed with one of the buddies in The Helen's. His buddies laughed at him, but he just up and did it. First he and Taffy got a suitcase from one of the rooms and stuffed it with old newspapers from the lounge of The Helen's.

"You can tell if someone's carrying an MT," Mik said to me later. "A guy forgets and hoists it," he illustrated, "so you got to stuff it." All he owned in the world were the clothes he arrived in: a khaki shirt, khaki trousers, sandals, not the fashionable kind. Sandals with holes in them, and buckled-down straps. Like children wear. That was all he had. Ben would have loved to have been so free.

In one of the newspapers was our ad, Jocelyn's and mine. We'd switched from the Female Only classified section to Men/Women. It was already two weeks old.

He borrowed a buck from Taffy. Then he humped the suitcase across the bridge. On the other side, he got a taxi to our house, with the buck.

"Your dumb sister!" he says to me. "She never even saw me drive up."

Jocelyn is a tall thin pre-Raphealite girl who moves through life in a Mr. Magoo way, miraculously avoiding all pitfalls and mud puddles. It is a family joke. One day she inadvertently became engaged to an Arab exchange student. "But we were talking about agrarian reform," she said wonderingly, after he had made a scene in Acadia camp. "He was telling me about his father's farms, and all I said was I would like to see them."

"I come up in a cab and does she see me?" Mik said. "Boy! Your dumb sister."

He knocked at the door and Jocelyn answered it. Yes, she said vaguely, we still had the room, nobody wanted it. You had to share the bathroom, she supposed that was why. It was just a sleeping room.

"What a salesman," Mik said. To me.

She took him upstairs. It was nice and bright, I'd cleaned it before going to West Vancouver, and it had new curtains. But it wasn't much, I guess. The bed cost ten dollars and the vanity, one of those elaborate three-way mirror things, was eight, from Love's auction. Jocelyn contributed the rug, a shag. There was a built-in cupboard arrangement for shirts and so on.

Jocelyn said to me later, "Do you think that was all right? Sixty-five?"

Mik has asked for board as well as room.

"I didn't think he'd go for the share system," said Jocelyn. We'd had actresses for a while and we shared everything four ways: food, rent, utilities. Our food never came to more than four dollars a week each.

"He asked for board too, so I said sixty-five," she said to me on the telephone. She was worried about making a profit. Neither one of us believed in landlord profits. "But I figure our time is worth something, cooking and putting up bag lunches and all that."

Mik said, with professional tenantese, "How about linen?"

"What? Oh, sheets, you mean? Okay. Sure."

"My personal laundry?" he said, pressing his luck.

"Oh sure, just throw it down the chute there. Don't leave the door open though, Sally got excited the other day and fell down."

"Unh?"

"Our cat. They were tearing around the place and she got excited and jumped into the laundry chute. She went all the way down. But it was okay, there was a whole week's wash down there. It was all right. It just scared her. Only we have to keep the chute door closed." She was worrying the problem of bag lunches. Mik had asked for board and she'd assumed this meant bag lunches, so she was trying to figure out the schedule. If she did his bag lunch when she did hers, which would be reasonable and efficient, what chore would I then swap? Jocelyn was scrupulously fair about housework. She hated it, and still does, going Slam Bam Thank You Ma'am through everything. She was wondering if it would be fair to ask me to do two breakfasts to her one for bag lunches every night. I drove her mad with my nit-picking. She did everything she was supposed to but I would wait eagerly for my turn at the kitchen, the wash, the bathroom, the floors, because now I could do it properly. She doesn't remember any of this. She says, "I don't remember you being so domestic." And, "I left under the kitchen sink for you," when I come to visit. "God, Vicky, you've changed a lot. You never used to be so fanatic." Our bedroom was schizophrenic. Jocelyn viewed it as not in the public domain and therefore never made her bed or put anything away. It was as though an imaginary line were drawn down the floor: on one side Dionysus rampant; on the other Athene couchant.

"I'm a clerk down at city hall," Mik said.

"Oh, that's nice," said Jocelyn. "I'm a student, but I'm working as a waitress 'till summer school. I have to go pretty soon."

But Mik was going to get the other part of the 'we' out of her. He'd gone this far and he wasn't going to stop now. He knew she couldn't be the real landlady.

"Your husband a student?" But he had looked at her hand.

"Oh I'm not married. I live with my sister."

"Oh, she's the landlady, your sister."

"We're both the landladies," said Jocelyn.

He waited in the dining room while she found the extra key.

He couldn't believe it. He had to say it, even if she didn't ask.

"Uh, I'm short right now but I'll pay you Monday."

"Oh sure." She hadn't even thought about asking for money.

"I mean," said Mik later, "I don't think she should be running around loose." Shaking his head. "Neither one of you should be running around loose."

We weren't very business-like, Jocelyn and I. One of the actresses had invited an actor to stay for the weekend and he'd remained for four months. At the end, Jocelyn said to me, in a cross voice — being materialistic always makes her cross; she has to get mad to do it — "I think we should ask John for *some*thing."

We decided that it wasn't fair to ask John to pay towards the rent as he was sleeping in the sun porch, which wasn't heated. But he should pay four dollars a week towards the food, or whatever it worked out to once he was chipping in. And, "Maybe he could do the furnace," I said.

The furnace. My God. All that bit about the wood stove up at the island. *I* could make a fire. Every day I got the furnace going. Well, then, what was I doing, letting Mik show me how to . . . Oh. Yes. Mik didn't know that I could make a fire. And I let him *show* me, helpless lady that I was.

Anyway. Jocelyn and I drew straws and I lost. John was quite pleased to pay four dollars a week, we should have asked before. He'd wondered once or twice. But he never did make up the furnace. They didn't have call until noon, and I start work early.

"Well," said Mik, "I'll just leave my suitcase upstairs then."

He walked back across the bridge in a euphoria of success, burst into the beer parlor at The Helen's and said, "I made it." They didn't believe him at first. Then he did a B & E and went on a five-day bash.

The West Van trip had ended rather disastrously for me. I'd rushed back that morning to see The Nut Lady. "You've got to put me away," I said.

Now I was seeing a therapist.

When Ben signed himself out of Essondale, I had a long talk with the doctor in charge. Crease I mean. Crease.

"You might need some supportive therapy yourself," he said.

"But what's wrong with him?"

"The prognosis is not good," he said. "He's a latent homosexual."

I didn't believe it. I still don't.

"We don't usually do this, especially if you yourself were to consider therapy, but we think you had better think about getting a divorce."

''Can't he get therapy?''

''We don't recommend it,'' the doctor said. ''But you might consider the clinic. It's free.''

Free. Yes, well, thank you very much but I pay my way. If it's free how can it be good? I thanked him very much and went back to the house.

In the mornings, Ben slept. Around noon he would get up and go down to the dining room where Francie was working on her correspondence lessons. Like me, she was exempt from public school because of ill health. Actually, she could have gone, but she hated the confusion. It was easier to whip all the lessons off in one fell swoop and then concentrate on life.

I was upstairs at the desk but I could hear snatches of the conversation:

''What you do is get hold of some potassium cyanide,'' Ben is saying, ''And then you put some in a tablet, one of those cylinder tablets you can put together. Then you get a lot of other tablets the same shape, colour, and you put them in a bottle and you take one a day, only they don't have anything in them, or maybe baking soda, and then that way it becomes habitual.''

''But how do you get hold of potassium cyanide?'' Francie says seriously.

''Yes. That's the problem. Vicky could have got it if she were still at the lab.''

And then there was the sure-fire bathtub method: ''But Ben, if you turn off the lights, you won't be able to see to get your wrists in position for the razor blades.''

''Oh yes, that's right,'' Ben says. This is the one where he gets into a hot bath so he can't feel a thing, and the machine comes, down, automatically, and *slice.* The lights had to be out so he couldn't see the water turning red.

Francie comes up from the States and I say to her, now, ''What else happened that fall? I can't remember clearly. What were Ben's great suicide plots?''

''Oh God, I don't know,'' and she laughs. ''Ben was great.''

''Great?''

''He was so funny, even about suicide. The Rube Goldberg variations. He was so great.''

''I can't remember. About his jokes. I know he was funny. But I can't remember. It's not fair, not to put in how funny he was. But I can't remember. What happened? I can't remember. How did you go? I don't even remember your going.''

''I had appendicitis. Don't you remember?''

''Did you? Did you have them out?''

''It. I had it out. Don't you remember? I had to go home. They went swish! and it popped out.''

''I don't remember. I can't remember about your appendix.'' And later, when she is having a bath, I go in to make sure. Yes. There's a scar.

''My God,'' I say.

''Well, you were pretty far away, that fall. What a weird time! And I'm coming out of the ether and the nurse says, ''How far gone are you, dear?'' Because I hadn't had my period for four months.''

''Oh that's right, what was his name?''

''Carlos Johnston,'' Francie says gloomily.

''Didn't I call the police because you were out late?''

''Yeah. Boy, was I furious. Don't you remember, Mom came out and took one look at him. Big black booger, and she whisked me home?''

''And he raped you,'' I say, feeling the old fear; the old guilt. I hadn't looked out for her.

But Francie doesn't answer this. ''What was I?'' She is sitting soaping her breasts in the tub. ''Was I fourteen or fifteen?'' We work it out. Fifteen.

When Jocelyn came home from class, Ben would tell her all over again.

At least, that's how I remember those months. I wore an 18½ size dress. I was enormous.

But Jocelyn's version is quite different. One day her creative writing instructor phoned me and told me she'd written ''a very interesting play. About you."

"Can I read your play?" I said to Jocelyn. She is cuddled up on the front room sofa with David. I am trying not to show how much this bothers me. Public displays of affection, ugh.

"No, Vicky. I couldn't."

So I sneak it. One day when she is out, I take it from her desk and I read it. It's lying right on top, she trusts me that much. On the cover it has "A" and "*Most* interesting."

Is that true, about Joss cuddling with David? No. They still don't. When he got home at Christmas, the most they did was touch each other lightly on the shoulder. David is even worse than me about public affection. It is all in my mind. They are just sitting there, but the charge is high.

It is called "Merry-Go-Round" and is all about a successful woman writer who lives in a big old house with her sloppy sister and her emasculated husband. She is beautiful and competent, and nags everyone about cleaning up the mess. Her husband sleeps all day and the beautiful writer comes into his room, picks up his canister of pencils and dumps them; crash! onto the floor. To wake him up. To make him feel guilty. When she isn't dumping canisters of pencils and nagging her sloppy sister, she is sitting at her typewriter going clackety-clack like a machine, making money. She keeps making logical statements with no regard for emotional truth. The husband brings her cups of tea. It is very funny and farcical and I would have given it an A too. Or an A minus anyway.

One day I hear Ben going on downstairs to both of them about the latest surefire way to do himself in. It fulfills all the requirements: it is painless, allows no reversal of decision, and does not leave a mess for anyone to clean up. I come downstairs like Armageddon.

"Look. Ben? Look. You just walk down to Granville Bridge and you just climb over the rail and you just push yourself off. I mean, I'm sick and tired of all this crap. If you want to do it, do it and get it over with."

They are all horribly embarrased for me. We don't know

what to do with violence. We just feel so ashamed for the person. They don't know where to look. Ben gives me a pitying smile. I register at the free clinic.

"I'm destructive," I say in my first session. "I told my husband to go jump off a bridge."

About a month later, I am saying, "You've got to get out, Ben. I'm destroying you." Full of disinterested concern, that's me. "I've talked to Ivan, he'll take you. Really, you'll be better off there." It is all arranged. He is to leave Friday.

"You keep the car, Vicky," says Ben.

"No, that's your car. You did the motor job."

"Then you keep the hi fi. And the cats."

"All right."

"After," he says, "after, you can have the car back." Meaning after he is dead.

On Friday morning I go out and stay away until noon. When I leave at eight the house is congealed. Francie and Jocelyn, where are they? I don't remember. When I get back, there is Ben, standing like a waif in the garden.

"I can't," he says.

"You have to," I say and go away for another four hours. When I get back, he is gone, and I am left with the hi fi and the thirteen cats. We did not believe in possessions. There was so little to divide.

Relief like a blessing pours through me. I go upstairs and work for a while. It is Jocelyn's turn to cook. At dinner, her eyes are puffy and red. Francie is in her bedroom. She won't come down.

"I had to," I say. "I had to."

"I know," Jocelyn says. "But you just go upstairs and you . . . you're like . . . it's like you've got a steel trap for a mind. It's like . . . ." and she stands there, her lips shaking. "I know you did. It's just . . . ." And she leaves the room.

I could never bear being unhappy. That was always my trouble. I'm still that way. If I'm unhappy I think something is terribly wrong.

I went upstairs and I wrote and I forgot all about Ben. I was trying to write a story about a man who commits suicide. About his family really. How they are, after. How they try to understand it.

"You've got to stop giving him money now," Jocelyn says later. That night. She has come down and said she was sorry. "Why can't he go on unemployment insurance?"

"He's not eligible. He's in the executive bracket or something."

"The exectuive bracket?" said Jocelyn. "But that means he must have made a lot of money when he was working."

"Oh I don't think so. It just means he was on the managerial side or something."

"What was he making?"

"I don't know. He never told me."

"Didn't you *ask*?"

"No. I never thought about it."

"God." We are drinking tea and there is a long pause.

"I sneaked your play," I say.

"What did you think?" Jocelyn says before she remembers.

"It's good. I liked it. It's very funny."

"Oh Jesus," she says. "Oh shit. Look. Vicky. It's not really true, you know. I mean, that's not the way I really see you. I mean, you make it up, you know. It starts one way and then you make it up to fit."

"The form takes over," I say. "I know."

But it is true. Everything you make up is true. Too.

"We'd better put an ad in," says Jocelyn. "Francie can sleep with me."

So we put an ad in and we get the actresses.

Francie leaves, though I don't remember how. Jocelyn goes to classes. The actresses go to rehearsal. I work on the suicide play. November 14. The day I would have had the baby. I go on a diet. I start to lose weight.

But that isn't how I remember it. I remember it more dramatically. I remember a great rushing wind pouring out of me. I remember going down like a balloon. I've had to put in the diet, because that is also true. It is a fact. But

Somewhere in there Ben registers for teachers' training.

One night I wake. It is black in the bedroom. I can hear them making love in the other bed. Jocelyn and David. I lie there, afraid to move, afraid to breathe. They are making love, groaning and panting. The bed springs are jerking violently. How can she? In the same room. I lie there petrified with horror and shame.

The Nut Lady says, "Are you sure?"

"I was right there."

"Have you asked your sister about it?"

"No! My god. How could I?"

"Vicky," she says, very gentle with me in these days, "didn't this happen before?"

"No. She's never done that before."

"Did you tell me about this before? When you were five? About your father and how he took your hands from your ears. How he said, "She's lying! She's awake. She's lying there listening."

"Dear god. Then I am mad."

"Talk to your sister," says the Nut Lady.

"No! My god, Vicky, how could you think I could do it! Or David! David's so square he can't even dance with me in public. No! It isn't true."

"I heard you. I heard the whole thing. It was real."

"I swear!" Jocelyn says.

"I know. I know. I know you weren't there. I know. I just heard you, that's all."

"What does she say it is?"

"Something called hypnogogic vision. Where you externalize."

"But why would you do something like that?"

"Daddy caught me listening once. Well, I was trying not to

listen, but he got mad at me. She thinks that's it."

Jocelyn says, after a while, "Does it happen often? Do you get these things often?"

"I don't know," I say. "That's the trouble."

But Jocelyn is still angry. "Well, if you want to *know*, we only do it when we're prepared to take the risk."

"What?"

"We only do it when we're willing to get caught," she says, her mouth tight, like my mother's. "That's what you believe, isn't it? That's what you think. You don't think it's right unless you get punished. Well, you can be satisfied about *that.*"

"What?"

"And we have never done it here, never!"

Oh Jocelyn. Oh my god.

43 year-old KEITH MAILLARD was born in Wheeling, West Virginia, and emigrated here in 1970. His novels include *Two Strand River* (1976), *Alex Driving South* (1980), and *The Knife In My Hands* in 1981. His most recently published work was *Cutting Through* (1982), and his latest novel, *Motet*, is scheduled for publication in the near future. He is also an accomplished and practising musician.

KEITH MAILLARD

an excerpt from the novel

Motet

Good morning, little schoolgirl — Pigpen's line, old hippy joke that Steve had been singing to himself for the last hour as he'd floated the van in a random search pattern through this tree-lined genteel neighborhood, giggling like a bona fide cretin getting off on the same dumb twist long after everybody else has given up on it and gone home. He rolled the window down and stuck his head out to catch the drift of the hazy rain, saw his own grin like the Chesy cat's fading away behind the gauze scrim of this nostalgic Chinese landscape painting, everything flat and featureless, the mountains nothing but paper cutouts, broad streets of mildew and missed connections, stucco boxy doll houses arranged neatly in a swamp, city of fanatical gardeners, six-inch slugs, and dripping conifers smelling of gin — Vancouver. Yeah, you come cheap these days, he thought, amusing yourself in the Taoist rice-paper void. Can't look it up in the phone book, no that'd be too easy for you — got to take off instead without even knowing for sure the part of town it's in and sniff it out on telepathy. But now he couldn't help grinning because he'd done it, pulled up to the curb just a half block up from the discreet sign, white letters on a natural wood ground — ALLENBY HOUSE SCHOOL FOR GIRLS — carefully placing the van between the entrance and the bus stop. Light a smoke now to help the twitch along, no problem, folks, just your friendly neighborhood child molester.

The building itself was invisible behind high square hedges so solid and dense and green and ancient they could have been growing since the reign of Elizabeth the One, courtier's labyrinth, and the only way in through that high wide archway. And you've made it right on time — procession of kidlets up the sidewalk past the van. They've let the little ones out first, and these were the babies of the mystery — pleated skirts, kneesocks, giggles and raincoats, toting satchels, ghosts of children distanced and muted like memory in the mists of February. So what is it, Steven? Twenty years of getting older and playing to girls who just keep getting younger so now you've got nothing left for it but to fabricate appointments at the school yard gate?

Steve lay back in the seat to drag smoke and listen to the continuous sifting of the rain on the roof. The bigger girls were on their way out now, and damn, he'd almost missed her. Yellow plastic raincoat and matching down-easter hat tied under her chin, made her look about ten, blending in with the other children, but the first giveaway was the big instrument case in her gloved hand, and then, of course, she turned her head and cast out a sweep of that impossible blond hair. Traitor's heart skipped a beat just like fourteen again, catching sight of some beloved Sally or Susie across the schoolyard — Romeo forever — and suddenly he wanted to take his hang-dog face and rancid fantasies and sneak away with them on the wet shame of his own predicament, put the van in gear and ooze past the water running in the gutters and keep right on going out into the middle of English Bay. Steven, you flaming asshole, sixteen, for Christ's sake!

"Hey, little schoolgirl, can I come home with you?"

Flash of blue eyes, flushed bird going up — scatter of wings — so far out to lunch she hadn't even seen the van. "Steven!"

"Ten years I've been waiting to deliver that line for real."

"Are you waiting *for me?*" she said like she couldn't believe it, little pop of a sentence she didn't catch quick enough.

I'm so waiting for you that the rest of the world's just stopped like Don Juan's trump card. "Sure. I'll take you home."

"Come on, Carla, he'll give us a ride," to her little buddy — a child, an absolute baby, no lie, not a curve in sight and black hair in pigtails for Christ's sake, and big suspicious eyes that were saying, *I* know all about men in vans.

"It's all right, Carla, I know him."

But Carla wasn't having any, not about to climb into any old rapist's wagon, had stopped dead with books clutched to her flat chest and panic written all over her, probably memorizing the details for the cops later, already telling herself the whole repulsive story — Wendy's messed-over white corpse dug up out of a shallow grave with dirt in the open eyes.

But Wendy shrugged, walked around to the other side, and climbed in, laid her books and fiddle case in the back.

"She going to run straight home and call your daddy?" Steve said under his breath.

Wendy gave him a quickly narrowing stare. "Yes, she might do just that," leaned across him to try it again. "Carla, it's all right. *I know him*. He's a friend of my father's. Do you want a ride?"

NO! mute Carla said with her head, but seemed slightly reassured, waved half-heartedly, lowered her pigtails and walked against the rain, stiff as a little mule. Steve put the van in gear and pulled away, careful and easy, drifting down the wet street, slow-motion getaway. "*Are* you going home?" he said.

"I *was* going home."

"What the hell you doing giving me your past tense, Gwendolyn?" That's it, man — light and easy, slow and breezy.

Pause. "I'm giving you anything you want with my past tense, Steven," said in that British deb voice.

Goose-bumped sweating pig, Steven Beuhl, stopped for a red light and lit a new smoke on the butt of the old. "Tell me how to get there."

"I'm serious, Steven."

"Wonderful. Delightful. Fantastic. Terrific. Tremendous."

"I don't want to go home. Seeing you is more important." Light changed, he pulled away, smoke in his throat and not a good word in his head. "Why didn't you call me?" she said.

"I know you well enough to call you?"

"You know me too well not to. I wasn't sure I was ever going to see you again."

"I wasn't sure you were either."

"I knew that's what you were thinking. I knew you wouldn't call. You could have at least called *Kathy*."

"Yeah, I could of, couldn't I? Where are we going?"

"I don't care. Anywhere you want."

"I don't know this damned city." And added, after a moment of sticky indecision, "Kathy knew where I was. I *did* call her."

"Well, she didn't tell me. You didn't expect her to, did you?"

"No."

"Why didn't you call me? I couldn't very well ask her about you."

"I'm glad you understand."

"Understand *what*, Steven?"

Stopped for another red light, he turned to look at her. Goddamn that child's rain gear, goddamn that hat tied under her chin and those mary janes and knee socks. Steven took it out on the van, kicked it down, tires squealing, fishtail and slam. "Steven!"

"Sorry. I'm a bit frazzed."

But you *can* hold it together, he told himself, wind it through the rain easy as a feather. "Where are you living now?" she said.

"Basement room in the East End."

"What are you doing?"

"What the fuck you think I'm doing? I'm playing in a rock band that's what I'm doing. Jesus Christ. Three lads from Nanaimo come down to the big city to make their hard-ass music. Larry, Phil, and Jim and green as the goddamned eighteenth hole. So green they can't tell the difference between yours truly and a sane man. So glad to get a wizard like me on drums that they pitched right in and cleaned out the root cellar to make me a bedroom. Wonderful little space. Used to be full of jam jars, you know, right next to the octopus furnace, conveniently located right off the backed-up sump in case I should decide to drown myself in the night. Oh hell. But it ain't a bad life. Beats the shit out of the black plague."

Long silence in the fuzzy rain. She wasn't laughing. And he sneaked a glance at her, at that perfect milk-white profile. She was looking straight ahead at the road. "Where the hell we going?" he said.

"The Endowment Lands."

"Tell me how to get there. It's your city."

"You're going the right way. Just keep going west. It doesn't matter how you go."

"Shit, kid, that's practically a koan."

"Steven? What's the matter with you? Do you feel bad about Kathy?"

"What the fuck do you think?"

"Stop it. Don't do that to me."

"Oh shit. Of course I feel bad about Kathy."

"You left her. You didn't call her. You didn't write to her."

"Damn it, don't you think I don't know that? Jesus Christ, Wendy."

"Is that what you do to everybody? Are you going to vanish again?"

"Just keep on going west, isn't that what you said? It doesn't matter how you go."

"Yes, it does matter. It matters to me."

"Who the hell are you to take it on, schoolgirl? Jesus!"

"Why were you waiting for me then?" And that was such a good question there was no answer for it at all.

"There ain't nothing here," he said. The Endowment Lands.

"That's right." Looked at her. Blue eyes like incoming flash across a million empty miles. "Drive on back through there,'' she said, pointing. ''Get out of view of the road.''

''Nothing but trees. Shit, Wendy, that's a sea of mud back there.''

''Go on.''

''Hey, I don't think it's a good idea.'' You're a fucking master of understatement, aren't you, candy man? Not a good idea? That goddamned warning note's ringing like somebody's kicking the gong around from one side of your skull to the other. Gong around, gong around, got to stop kicking the gong around. *Stop it, man, all right? Just stop it.* ''Jesus, Wendy, it's raining like a son-of-a-bitch. There's not going to be anybody out in those woods. Nobody for miles. I'm going to take you home.''

''You're not going to take me home.'' She dropped one gloved hand over Steve's on the steering wheel.

Her kid gloves. Black ones today, a long pair. ''Shit, you run across some man with a glove fetish, you'd drive him bananas.''

''My hands get cold very easily. I never thought of gloves as sexy, but I guess they are, aren't they? I'm glad that at least *something* I do is sexy. Go on, Steven, get us off the road.''

Gong around, gong around, got to stop kicking that gong around. Steve eased the ticking van back through the tall green trees, turned off the ignition, ca-bang, ca-bang, ca-bang from the engine, a drummer that couldn't quit. Got to run, got to move. And he felt the treacherous seat begin to move under him, very gently, like ripple in a waterbed. The pressure on his head was enormous.

''You're not going to convince me,'' she said.

''What the fuck are you talking about?'' Strained door-spring voice coming from somebody else. He lit a cigarette. His hands were shaking. Gong around, rain rain, gong around, rain rain.

''You're not going to convince me you're a worm. And I'm no rose either.''

The pressure was a huge hand, was the roof of the van, but there wasn't any escape from it. Outside it'd be in the rain, in the sky itself. Steve bent and pressed his forehead into the steering wheel. Talking to the dashboard, talking to his bony knees. "Can't you tell the difference between me and a human being? Jesus, kid, you take chances."

"I'm not taking any chances."

"If that's what you think, then I'm going to take you home." He reached for the key in the ignition, but she caught his hand. Moist leather on his bare skin.

"You're shaking," she said.

He couldn't look at her. He was cold, clenched his teeth against it. "You're in over your head, baby. You don't know who you're dealing with."

"And you don't know who you're dealing with." She held out a hand to him. Break.

The girl was wearing black kid gloves. Steve didn't take the hand, but drew farther back into himself, impacted. He felt as detached from his body as if he were floating a foot in the air above it, watching. He watched himself squeeze his arms tightly around his chest so the shaking couldn't rip him apart.

The man needed to press his back into the seat. The cold rain-colored daylight hurt the man's eyeballs just under the ridge of skull, thumb on bruise. The pressure on the man's head was enormous.

The girl was white and shining. The green west blurred, but the girl in focus, shining. "Steven, you're not lost forever."

The man could hear the tremendous effort in the girl's flat voice, the forced control. The girl untied the rain hat from under her chin, pulled it off, and dropped it onto the floor at her feet, shook out damp straight hair.

The man felt the seat under him moving deeply now, a tide of motion. He squeezed his elbows into his chest until he was compressed, compacted, a pinched black iron pipe. Then he exploded. Smashed open door, metal slam at the wind, jumped into rain. He was running through the alien green trees.

You're out of the van, slapdash down the trail, pin green smear, that nothing of sky, hemmed in, claustrophobic green bent toward the middle, curving, coming down, bent around your ears. "Steven!" she's yelling, a skimming owl behind you, a long float through the slashing rain. Run, push against the knife in your side, feet tangled in mud, leaf mulch. Bang into tree, turn, make her human again. See a little kid in a yellow plastic raincoat, her socks coming down, her legs splashed with mud all the way to her knees. She stops ten feet away, and you stare at each other. She's panting and you're panting, run half a mile up the trail but come out nowhere, see no way out at all, just more trees, enormously, going on forever. Press your back into the bark, panting. She could run you down with no trouble, but she doesn't try to come close, stops on the other side of the trail, presses her back to a tree. You're lined up like two chess pieces. "Steven, listen, you've got to listen."

"No." But you can listen. The thing that comes and runs you has gone away for now.

"I don't care whether you want to or not, you've got to." If you tilt straight back and let the rain pound you full in the face, it makes the sockets of your eyes fill up with water, you blink, the water burns, and there's a patch of sky up there, rolling ink grey, between tree tops. "Let me alone, Wendy. Go away."

"No. Listen. I was asleep. I didn't know that I was asleep. Do you hear me? I woke up and it had all been sleep, fifteen years of sleep. I woke up in Amsterdam. I didn't know it was going to happen. We got off the plane, and the airport just looked like any other airport, and I thought: oh, is this all? And then I knew that I'd been expecting something to change. It felt like something very fragile I was carrying in my hands. I had to balance it very carefully, walk very carefully, but I knew I was expecting something. And I thought: Oh, is this all? It's just another airport. It could be Toronto or Vancouver."

"I don't want to hear it."

"I don't care. You've got to hear it. And then later I thought, Yes, it's here after all. It *is* going to happen. It was when I saw the canals, the old parts of the city, the cobblestones. Daddy and I went to a hidden church. They had to hide it because of the persecution. And I thought, It's happening."

Hammering in your ears like an endless press roll. "What's it got to do with me? Why the fuck you want to tell it to me?"

"Shut up, Steven. We went to the house where Anne Frank stayed, and I felt it. . . inside my chest. It began to hurt inside my chest, and I knew it wasn't something I was carrying in my hands, it was inside of me, that very fragile thing. It was going to open up, and I thought, I've been asleep. I've been asleep for fifteen years."

"I don't want to hear it."

"Shut up. Daddy took me out to Klaas Achterberg's. He lives outside the city. The land is unbelievably flat, and every inch of it is cultivated and the sky. . . My God, Steve, the sky is everywhere. It's huge. It was raining that day, overcast and drizzling, a kind of grey drift of rain. It was like the paintings in the Rijksmuseum. And everything was hurting me then. Everything I looked at hurt me. The sky hurt. The flat countryside hurt. And I had a lesson with Klaas. We read some Marais. I played it and then he played it, and I *heard* it for the first time. I knew what it was supposed to sound like for the first time. He's such a funny round little man. He doesn't look like anything. He could be a farmer. . . that's what he looks like. But then he plays, and the music just comes pouring out. . . as though it were coming up out of a deep fountain. And I knew how stupid I was, how I couldn't really make *music*. I knew that all I'd been doing had been playing the notes. And then Daddy and I walked for hours afterward and it was still raining.

You're hooked, you're a shining silver fish jumping on tense wire, and now you've got to know. The rain's soaked your hair, it's running in your face. You wipe it out of your eyes to see her. She's a girl in a yellow raincoat standing ten feet away. She's shaking with cold. She sees you look and takes a step forward. "Stay where you are, all right? Just stay right there."

She stops, draws back. "Daddy talked to me in a different way than he ever had before. He talked to me as though. . . . It's hard to describe. For a while I wasn't his daughter, I was . . . not just a friend. More than a friend. I was his colleague, something like that. He told me all kinds of things I never knew about him. He told me about the first woman he ever slept with. He told me about studying with Thurston Dart in London. He told me about how he'd wanted to play early music, bring it to life again, and I couldn't say anything to him. I just walked. I felt like the sky, big and flat and grey. I couldn't say anything at all because it was opening up inside of me, and I knew I'd been asleep. I kept thinking about when I was a little kid. Mummy used to dress me up and take me to concerts, and I was asleep. I used to play my cello, and I was asleep. I got up every day and went to school, and I was asleep. And I kept thinking, I've got to remember. If I don't remember, it'll slip away again. It was the most horrible thing I could think of. . . for it to slip away again. But I couldn't stand the pain inside of me. Mummy and Cindy would be out somewhere, and I'd tell Daddy, 'I've got to take a nap. I'm really tired,' and I'd go into my room and cry. It hurt so badly that I had to cry, but I didn't want it to stop hurting. Because if it stopped hurting, I'd just be asleep again. I thought, I've got to keep the pain . . . as though it were something sharp to press myself up against whenever I had to. Because if I lost it . . . . Do you understand? You've got to understand."

"Goddamn it, of course I understand."

"I wanted to stay in the Netherlands. I wanted to spend the whole vacation there. I wanted Mummy and Cindy to go on to Italy and for Daddy and I to stay in Amsterdam, but I couldn't even say it. There wasn't any way to say it. All the plans had been made. We were going to rent a car and drive to

Paris. But then everything got changed, and I knew something terrible was going to happen. I couldn't say anything. I just watched, and everything started going wrong. Cindy and I were picking at each other all the time as though we were both five years old again, and Mummy and Daddy were fighting, and everything was going sour, and I couldn't do anything about it. Part of me was just *watching*, and I'd act like a spoiled little bitch, and Cindy would act worse, and we'd be yelling at each other, and Mummy would be yelling at us, 'My God, will you girls stop it! You're driving me crazy.' And I'd watch and think, Wendy, why are you doing this? But I couldn't stop it. And then we decided to go to Antwerp . . . . I don't know any other way to tell it, Steven. Just like this. . . all the trivial details one right after the other. It feels as though I have to tell you all the silly trivial details."

"Yeah, you've got to do that."

"Daddy wanted to follow the route of the Netherlandish composers down into Italy, but he didn't tell Mummy that, he just said, 'I think we can pass on Paris this time,' but she really wanted to go to Paris and so did Cindy. Cindy had the idea that she was going to get her hair cut in Paris, you know, *styled in Paris*, and she wanted to buy some French clothes, but Daddy had decided that he wanted to go to Antwerp, and then over into Germany, down through Switzerland, and into Italy. He told Mummy, 'Well, we've never been to Antwerp and we have been to Paris. We've never been to Bonn either,' and he told her about the Rubens paintings in Antwerp, so she gave in. I didn't want to go to Antwerp. I didn't know why. I just didn't want to, but I couldn't say a thing.

"I kept thinking how modern the highway was. We drove straight to Antwerp, and everybody was fighting all the way. When we came into the city my heart sank because it was so big and modern and dirty-looking. . . like Hamilton, I guess. And I thought, It's ruined. They've ruined it. And Dad just wanted to stop at a motel. . . they have motels, you know, just as in North America. . . but Mummy said, 'No, we'll get to a good hotel,' and she was allowed to win that one because she hadn't wanted to go to Antwerp in the first place. So we stayed in a big hotel that was right on the river. The Schelde. And we looked at the Rubens paintings. I hate Rubens.''

You've got to laugh at that one. ''Oh, you do, huh?''

''Yes. He's too flamboyant. Too showy. But we had to look at all of his paintings we could find. And we went to the cathedral. It's really huge inside, but you don't realize it at first. We walked around. There were two more damned Rubens paintings in there, and we had to look at them, and by then the pain was so bad that I didn't think I could stand it. It started down in my. . . started right between my legs and went right up to the top of my head. It felt as though I were being ripped apart, and I had to fight it all the time. It gave me a headache to fight it like that, and Mummy said 'Oh, she's got one of her migraines,' and they sent me to bed. And I lay there and I was thinking, Yes, that's what she thinks of me. To her I'm just a spoiled, pampered, little bitch of a kid. I cry for no reason. I have migraines. I get sick at my stomach and throw up. I'm like the princess who can feel the pea under all the mattresses. That's exactly what she thinks of me, and she hates me for it because that's what she was like when she was a girl. But I thought, I'm not really like that. I'm not like that at all. That's just what I *look* like. It comes from being asleep for fifteen years.

''They brought me something to eat, but I couldn't eat it, and I saw Mummy looking at me with that expression she gets, and I knew she was thinking, 'Oh, you fucking little bitch, I'd like to strangle you,' and then they all went to bed. They were in one room and Cindy and I were in another, and I kept twisting around in the bed because the pain kept getting worse. I couldn't cry because Cindy was there. It was the worst pain I've ever felt in my life. And then, all of a sudden, it stopped. It was just gone, and I felt this huge open space. I wasn't frightened at all. I thought, this is what I've been waiting for. And a voice said to me, 'You have to go out by the river.' So I got up and got dressed. Cindy woke up and looked at me and said, 'What are you doing? I'll tell Mummy,' and I said to her, 'Cindy, if you tell Mummy, I'll make your life so miserable you won't be able to believe it,' and I looked at her so she knew I meant it. She said, 'All right. I won't.'

"It was just dawn, and I walked along the Schelde. I knew it was dangerous for me to be alone, but I didn't care. I stopped to look at the water, and the big open space got even bigger. It was like a vacuum. And then it started filling up. It was like liquid flowing down from the sky, a thick liquid comind down. It started with a single drop, and then it kept on coming until it filled everything. It was blood.

"It all filled up with blood, and I stood and waited, and the voice said, 'See how Christ's blood streams in the firmament,' and I said, 'I see.' "

"Shut up, Wendy. I don't want to hear any more of it."

"You've got to hear it. You don't have any choice. And then the blood parted like a curtain, and behind it was whiteness the color of milk. And the voice said, 'This is how it was in the beginning of all things,' and I said, 'I see.'

"And then a form began to take shape very high. It was like a swirl in the milk, and then it took a shape and a form. It was like a feather. It came floating down very slowly, and it was a piece of paper all rolled up. It glowed like the sun. And the voice said, 'Read what is written,' and it fell at my feet. I picked it up and opened it, and it said, 'You will speak to the peoples,' and then the paper burst into flames and turned to ash in my hands, and everything turned dark around me, and then I was frightened for the first time. I was terrified. And I knew I could die. And I thought, I don't want this. I don't want this to be happening to me. I want to be just an ordinary little girl. I felt very little. I started to cry. I thought, I'm only fifteen. I haven't had a chance. I don't want this to happen. And then I was standing by the river Schelde in Antwerp. It was just dawn, and the birds were singing everywhere, and I was frightened and ran back to the hotel, and I thought, I'll never tell anyone. I can't tell anyone. I want to go home. I want to go back to Vancouver, because it's my home, and I just want to be invisible. I just want to go to school and play my gamba and grow up and go off to college or get married or something and be safe. I just want to go home and be safe."

ROBERT HARLOW was born in Prince Rupert in 1923 and was educated at U.B.C. after earning the D.F.C. as a Flying Officer in the R.C.A.F. during World War II. He was Director of Radio, British Columbia, for the C.B.C. for ten years and was subsequently founder and head of the U.B.C. Creative Writing Department where he continues to teach. His five published novels include the trilogy *Royal Murdoch, A Gift of Echoes,* and *Scann*. His most recent fiction, *Paul Nolan*, appeared in 1984.

ROBERT HARLOW

Heroes

The house was two storeys, but David lived mostly in the top one, and he had refurbished it over the years so that there were now three rooms, two bedrooms and a study, upstairs. The study was large — twenty by twenty — and it overlooked English Bay, where today fifteen ships were anchored in the roads waiting for service at Vancouver's docks. He worked here at home now, did his design sketches, his reports and memoranda, and he waited on his father who was in bed in the spare room. A death watch. The old man was eighty-five and had a collapsed lung. Most certainly he was dying. Quite suddenly, sometime in the last couple of weeks, he'd begun to have no use for life. Perhaps he had decided; and if he didn't go today, he would tomorrow or next week. David had expected to feel distressed, at least saddened, but what he felt was privileged. Many of his friends simply got telegrams. Here, now, he was being instructed once again by his father, being led by him to the edge, at least, of one of the mysteries. It was an odd moment in his life, because at the same time there was Peggy happening. He could think of no other way of putting it.

He looked out over the top of his drawing board at the water. It had sunshine in it today and so it was green. Water birds were there near his shore ducking for food in the shallows. A pair of coots swam anxiously by. A half dozen mallards began that controlled panic which would eventually become flight, and then they settled back in the water without having gone anywhere. They began to feed again. This continual switch from the mindless to the purposeful was no more insane than what he was doing. He smiled. Life is risk. And what else? Loud desperation. But he was comfortable in retreat from the city, here five minutes from the heart of it.

His father seldom called on anyone for help, and he wouldn't accept assistance of any kind from anyone who wasn't family. When he'd first gotten bronchitis, months ago now, he'd been taken to the hospital, where he'd yelled and banged, turned up his radio to a howl, refused drugs, until doctor Billings had shrugged and said, "What can we say, he's not going to get well here, is he?"

It had been inconvenient to bring his father here from the hospital and to look after him most of the time by himself. His office did its best to accommodate him, but inevitably the arrangements were inefficient. Many architects were starving for work; even he wasn't doing all he could at the moment. And, beyond that, as if he were trying to bury an old life under new concerns, he had begun recently — made a decision — to commit himself to a relationship with Peggy and, this time, to be quite honest about it, to celebrate his fiftieth year with a new maturity and stop being a loner, a challenge to women and an enigma to men. How much this new beginning with Peggy grew out of his father's final illness he couldn't be sure, but he knew that the healthy energy she helped create in him made him think rationally about the dying that was going on in the other room.

Even so, the decision to bring his father here to look after him had not been made without emotion. He'd begun to take the old man back to the house in Dunbar where he'd lived by himself for the last eight years. A nurse — expensive as she was to be — was to live in. But sending him there became suddenly a selfish act. This was his *father,* and this was a time when they had to be together. David had brought him here and had arranged for a Helpful Aunt to come from an agency when he had to go to the office for meetings with clients or with his partners. He didn't mind nursing the old man, which was good, because what he felt for him left him no other choice.

He got up from his drafting table and switched off the stereo. Phil Woods' "Musique du Bois" was finished. The virtuosity of Woods' saxophone always left him stunned by the depth and breadth of its perfection; it was what technical grace allowed in art and was unknown in life, and it was what he struggled for in his own work.

Downstairs, he heard a key in the door and then: "Hello there," Peggy's voice called, kind, caring.

But he wondered — not wanting to — Do I have a name? Hello there. No, perhaps only an age. If she were honest — and she was in every other way — she'd call up to him, "Hello, fifty," and he would call back, "Hello, thirty-three." The routines of this deathwatch had made his mind niggardly at moments when he wanted to be most generous.

He shouted down to her how good it was that she was here. He always said that. It was true. The pressure of his feelings for her forced his breathing to become shallow and his diaphragm sponge. He stood by the door to his father's room and heard her say, "I've brought a different wine." There was something different too in her voice, mischief maybe.

"What?"

"I'll bring it up."

He turned to look in on his father. He was small, wasted now that he had fluid in his lungs. "I've forgotten," he said. His breath rattled.

"What is it, Dad?"

"I want to go home. How do I get there?"

"You're here now. Look, it's just up the hill. When you get better I'll take you there. I remember."

After a moment, the old man's eyes focussed again. "Was that the therapist coming in? I don't want her pounding my chest." He was going deaf, but he hated the therapist enough to hear her.

"No, she's already been this morning."

His father remembered and began suddenly to cry. David sat down on the bed and held him as close as he was allowed. The sobs came out like barbed wire. "If I was a horse," his father said in a tough old voice, "I'd just go out behind the barn and get well. Or not.'' He pushed himself away, back down onto the pillows.

Peggy was at the door now. She had on a denim skirt that longed to be above her knees but wasn't. She'd been brought up in minis. Sandals on her precise feet. No bra. Her hair was simply cut, and short. It already had a few grey strands in it, which gave him hope — a particular clarity on the subject of aging; people *do* grow old at different rates.

She smiled at him and he went to her. She tipped her head to him. She loved her face to be kissed. But first he bent close to her ear and told her he loved her. It made him feel fierce, and he pressed his mouth down on hers. It gave way and their tongues met; finally the noise her lips made was a real kissing sound. It was part of her nature that she did everything well, even meticulously, but the sound of her kiss was the sound of someone loving. He hugged her and laughed quietly with her. He knew what they were doing, and especially what he was doing. After three grown children, a divorce and five years of chilly encounters with maybe a dozen women, he was open enough now to love. As simple as that. The plan to be a lover had taken over his life. Now he wasn't trying anymore to love; he was, in fact, loving. And it occurred to him that he had never done this before, or understood it if he ever had. It was as if he were inventing himself over again, minute by minute, and along with the invention went the power to direct those parts of the world his new dimensions touched.

When he first saw her, he decided she had shoulders Greta Garbo would have been jealous of, and her eyes smiled better than anyone else he'd ever known. He had seen her often at the desk in the science section of the main library, and finally — as with other affairs — he'd asked her to come and have a drink with him after work. The routine had begun as usual, but it had turned out differently. After a while, when it was time to go to bed, he could not make love with her in the way he had with others. It was embarrassing, cornball; loving her had stopped his athletics. He'd tried to laugh at it, but she hadn't joined in.

Kind, firm, serious, she'd said, "I think it's a generational thing, David. Sex for us is important — like enough money and a few good friends." Then she'd told him the story about the first months of loneliness and deprivation after she'd separated from her husband; finally she'd gone to a pub where she knew old friends might be and had taken one home. There had been quiet understanding, no questions. Good sex. It had restored her.

"Restored what?" he'd asked. He had no good sex for her, and now he was asking questions.

"It made me friendly with myself again," she'd said.

So, at least *there* they were opposites. For her it was not the act of love but loving itself that made her anxious and wary. He knew it wasn't a generational thing, but he was puzzled because he'd been converted, as if loving and commitment were a religion, and he wondered why she wasn't running to his church.

"I don't want to be hurt again," she'd told him. But it wasn't just that for her, any more than turning sex into pure love was seminal for him.

Now she drew away from his hug. "How's your dad?" she asked. She had a fine human concern for his father. Her own had died when she was fifteen.

"He's okay." He caught himself shrugging. "Doing what he has to do."

"You're so good with that old man," she said, and hugged him again, fierce, as if it were something she needed to know about him.

He looked over his shoulder at his father; his lashless eyes were closed. "Sometimes we talk about him as if he weren't here."

She left him and went to the side of the bed. The old man came awake again and looked at her. He flinched. "My God, Ellie, you're not supposed to be here."

"I'm not Ellie," she said earnestly.

He shook his head and his jaw worked. ''It's not right.'' He paused. ''Huh? No, I hear. What if they knew? Well, they do know. Everybody knows everything all the time, and that's the truth. They just won't say. Or damn well can't.''

David went to the other side of the bed. Peggy sat across from him and held his father's hand close to her chest. ''It's okay,'' she said. ''It's going to be okay.''

David leaned closer, suddenly affected by being with them both, but at another level in his mind there was a picture of them together, his father alive and there were no conditions — no dying, no anxious distress — and what was happening was so free and loving that they had put everything in their lives in balance. ''He's frightened,'' he said to Peggy quietly. ''I think that's what sends him back to where it's at least safer. Then he comes to and for a moment he doesn't know where he is and his mind reacts.''

''He doesn't look to me like he's somewhere safe.'' She bent forward and kissed the old man's forehead.

Together they watched his eyes, still fearful. David touched him, felt bones beneath slack skin and, fierce now too, hugged him again. ''Hey, come on,'' he said. ''We're here for you.''

She rested against him as he held his father. She put her head on his shoulder and her lips were close to his ear. He felt it strongly: ''I love you,'' he said.

After a long while, she said. ''And I you.'' There was a curious formality in her that he also loved, because beauty needs that too, as well as spontaneity — and perhaps a flaw.

''Get off me,'' his father said. He was back here again, and his glistering eyes looked up at hers once more but this time reflectively. His lips rose up off his yellowed teeth to make a tentative but mischievous smile. ''I bet you smell good,'' he said.

''Oh, she does, Dad, she really does.''

''Don't be an old coot,'' she told him, laughing.

''How do you feel?'' David asked him.

His eyes, dim now, wavered, their dance finished. He said,

"I can't hear or see or taste or smell anymore, but I feel no different inside than when I was nineteen." It was the truth, and it hurt him as much as it did his audience. He reached out and found their hands to hold. David listened for more, but that was as far into the mystery as the old man could take him. Beyond that knowledge there was surrender, loss — a private agony. His father grimaced, laughed, and then he released them both from being here, from having to be close.

They rose from the bed together and began to murmur those words that are part of the rigid ceremony of leaving the sick and dying, but he wasn't through with his moment of clarity. It obviously pleased him to be back in present time, to notice, to be a person again. "We lived nearly downtown then," he said to Peggy. "Near enough as dammit. In the West End there, not far from the water, either." He pointed. "And this young fella here was the most rational person I ever knew. When he was maybe three years old I'd come home from work and he'd be gone, his mother frantic. But I always knew where he'd headed; the docks if he could make it, the ships, and I'd find him blocks away. He'd never be surprised or try to run, and I'd fall in beside him and we'd talk. I never had to argue with him. We'd discuss the situation, how far it was to the boats, how close it was to dinner time, how come the sidewalk was flat and the buildings were so high, and he'd finally say, 'Time to go home,' and we'd walk it together back to his mother."

It was hard, suddenly, to control the muscles at the back of his throat. They bunched and cut off air. David coughed and laughed, rubbed his nose and eyes as if they itched. There was nothing to say. This was not a conversation. There had been, back there, trust. Love. His father was letting him (and Peggy too) know there had been loving, that he had broken through to it again himself, and now his dying was letting him tell it as if it were only a family story. There had been more than simply respect and father-and-son ties. And now the memory of it, and the effort of saying it, had again forced his father away from consciousness. Quite suddenly he slept his rattletrap sleep once more.

He followed Peggy out of the bedroom and into the study, connecting up as he went what his father had given him with what he felt for her. Where those feelings joined in him they became identical: love for his father, for her, for himself were one enterprise. The shock of finding regard for himself, after so long thinking he was a failure and unworthy, pleased him.

Peggy, in the middle of his study, turned, her eyes full of tears, and he held her again. She raised her face — as if holding her were a cue — to be kissed. "He's a dear old man," she said.

"He tried to tell you: he's not old — just his body," and again there was too much pressure at the back of his throat to breathe properly. He kissed her and hugged her hard. "Christ, old age is a coffin, and you're still alive when you're nailed into it." He felt her shiver, and he wished he hadn't said what had been in his mind.

"Who's Ellie?" she asked.

He shrugged. "Someone back there sixty, seventy years ago."

"A girlfriend?"

"Somebody not supposed to be here."

"Here? Or back there?"

"Back there is as much now as today is. For everybody. Surely you know that too?" He heard an edge of exasperation in his voice.

She shook her head. "I don't think I do."

Yet, he thought. He let her go. Then he saw what she had brought with her when she'd come. On his coffee table was a large bottle of sunshine-coloured wine.

She watched him see it. "Retsina," she said, and picked it up from beside two fat, short-stemmed wine glasses. "I love it," she told him, her mood changed now. Or perhaps she had only dismissed his. Her eyes were still serious.

"You never said."

She took the already-loosened cork from the bottle and poured.

"Now I'm saying it. Here, drink with me."

He held his glass. "Us," he said, toasting.

"Close friends," she said, as always, and drank.

He'd never found a taste for it. It was not wine. It was harsh. It had an odour, not a bouquet. It was rough, like real life, and the escape in it was not promised, only delivered, like a blow. "Why do you like this stuff?"

She smiled then and took his arm to lead him to the sofa by the windows. The light in the water had changed; it had made the green darker. A great blue heron floated east against the breeze and then pulled up sharply to land on a deadhead a hundred yards out from the shore. He looked at her and drank again. "It's tough stuff."

"It's not cloying," she said. "There's no expertise needed. Maybe you have to forgive it a little, but that's good for the soul." She put her hand out and touched him on the arm. "I can't stay."

"But this is your day off." He watched her. She had come, bearing wine, to say she couldn't stay: a kiss, a nod, a wave.

"I promised I'd relieve Kathy at the library this afternoon so she can get an early start on the weekend."

He drank from his glass, and waited; there was more.

"Then I'm going to be with Peter." Her eyes never wavered.

"Again?" he asked.

She nodded. "He left a message at my place. He needs me."

He felt ice form in his groin, and under his heart.

His father called: "Is anyone there?"

"Yes," he shouted back, and then realized that wasn't enough. He had to get up and go to him. The linen handkerchief he insisted on having to cough into was missing. It was under the pillow instead of up the sleeve of his pajamas.

When he went back to the sofa, she said, "Why do you do it? There are nurses and nursing homes." She had never asked before.

He said, "Does it bother you?"

She nodded. "Sometimes I think you're being melodramatic,

doing it all yourself."

"Do you think so?" He stood up, not quite knowing why, and then he went and picked up the retsina bottle from the table to pour more wine. "He has a right to die with dignity."

"I know," she said, "everything does. But what you two are doing, it's so — what? I don't know. So close."

He watched her sip her wine. Closeness hobbled freedoms and stifled liberation. He glanced away from her. One of the ships in the bay had weighed anchor and was moving slowly astern. He watched it.

"I'm glad if that's what you want," she said. Her voice was gentle, quiet. "You've taught me some things about love I didn't know in these past three months."

"My God," he said, laughing, "has it been that long?" He turned again to look at her. With her head tilted back and her eyes soft, she was beautiful. "Have I really taught you about love?"

She nodded. "It's so important to you. I keep hearing you say there's a place we can get to where there's a kind of love that makes people see each other as more important than anything else. I think I believe that now."

"It's natural to love." He tried to say it lightly

"I'm not used to it," she said. "With Peter —"

"What?"

"We had good times, good sex." She shook her head. "He left *me* alone." She got up and put her glass on the table. "I'll call you."

"When you get home from Peter's?"

"Yes. I don't know what time."

He plunged. "Are you having sex with him?"

She didn't hesitate, but her voice was cool. "I don't talk to him about us — that — and I'm not going to talk to you about me and Peter."

"Which means you do —"

"Not necessarily."

He tried to think what to say that wouldn't betray his age and be despairingly funny. "Am I supposed to think about myself that I don't share very well?"

She came back to him and put her hands against the sides of his head and raised her face to be kissed once more. He started to, but then she laughed lightly and said, "Isn't this life, though?" Her eyes pleaded with him to accept even that as real. "Smile," she said. "I just made a metaphysical joke."

"Did you?" David took her hands away from his face and looked over the top of her head so he could try to think clearly. "I want to tell you how I feel." He waited. She didn't move to leave. "I don't know what's going on. I'm the one with no control over the situation." He looked into her face again. "I'm the only one in love."

She nodded again; not, he knew, agreeing with him, but trying to hear what he was saying. "Peter and I are still married. You asked me to say good-bye to him, but I couldn't. Not yet. I need time. This is what I have to do."

"Goddamn," he said. "I feel like I'm being punished for good behaviour. What's this all about?"

But she didn't stay close. She went to where she'd dropped her coat and put it on. "It's about three people trying to be gentle with themselves and each other. I wouldn't blame you if you couldn't hang in while I get this straight for myself."

"How'd you feel if I quit?" He was plunging again.

She came back and stood close. "Relief," she said, finally. "A little relief." She was watching his face. He could see her looking for a reaction, but he waited. "And a great loss. A terrible loss." Her eyes kept searching.

"It's a desert you're going back to. What you learned here from being part of us you're going to take to him — as a god-damed gift — to make that desert bloom."

"It wasn't a desert. And in two years he's grown. So have I. We're seekers. We're still growing. Goddamn you yourself. Maybe you've quit growing, or done all you can. You're wonderful. You're a beautiful man . . ."

After a moment, he said, knowing the truth in his head when he heard it: "But that's all."

It was then that she kissed him with no holding back. "Hug," she said. "I need a hug." Then she looked up. "And I need us to be friends."

"I *do* want to support —"

She put her hand over his mouth. "I've *got* to go, okay?" But she went back across the room to his father's door and disappeared inside it. "You precious old man," he heard her say. "I love you."

And his father laughed. "You can come and pound my chest any time." His voice was steady and alive, younger.

She came back to the study, smiling, and saw David again. "I like him because he's so damned cute," she said. "Please, don't look like that." She gestured toward the bedroom. "He won't die just now."

She wasn't going to understand. He walked to the head of the stairway and held her there once more.

"Just give me time," she said. "This is what I have to do. This is who I am at the moment. All I can do is try to live in present time. As me."

"There's seventeen years between us," he said.

"And sometimes you want to be my parent," she told him. "Don't. Just let me go and be me." The reiteration hurt. She held up her face to be kissed. He touched her cheek with his hand, but didn't kiss her. His gut pained and then went hollow with fear. She said one final thing, already turning, "If it can't work out in the end, *you* will know you've not done one thing that's been negative or hurtful. You'll know that and be able to move on."

"But we can work it out," he said. "Phone me." And she nodded again and was gone with her own particular grace. He returned to the window. The freighter that had been moving astern was now gone. He put the stereo on again. Woods played his horn, and that was a different kind of grace: no commitment needed to share in it.

It occurred to him — as it had before many times — that he didn't know what Peter looked like. What did a man look like whose attraction was that he left her alone? Adonis. He'd have to be that. Someone ugly would need closeness.

That, of course, was not good enough. He listened to Woods: the savage rip of his music in its lower register. He sat on the sofa, poured a full glass of Greek wine and drank. He waited for the retsina's fist to deliver its own rough escape. Nothing happened. He heard his father cough, and thought again about the time he would go to him and he would be gone. All gone. Relief, then loss. That would be if he were not there. If he were lucky, he'd be there when the old man died. Throes, they called those last minutes — not a simple folding up or a gentle closing off. David got up and went into the bedroom and sat in the chair by his father's bed. The old man was asleep.

She might come back. He stood up as if he'd heard her returning. He left his father and went into the other room. But the door didn't open and the phone didn't ring. Across the bay he could see an office tower he'd designed. For a moment he wanted that to count. Peter was a librarian. Do librarians, for God's sake, *have* good times, good sex? Peggy was also a librarian. He went back toward his father's room. The alternatives were to love or simply to react. He pushed at the chair and it banged up against the side of his father's bed. "But really there is no choice," he said out loud.

"What're you doing?" the old man asked.

"Being a goddamned hero."

"Whatever that means." His father was lucid again.

"It means being stuck with doing what's right."

"For that girl?"

David laughed and sat on the bed. Then he held the old man's hand and let out the anger. "I'm stuck — not with love, that's too damned easy — but with loving: support, caring, kindness."

"That's a real bitch," his father said, and even his eyes were clear now. "But I don't suppose I'll be bothering you much longer.''

''Not you.''

''Not her. Not me. Who?''

He sat back down in the chair, knowing he didn't have to answer, that his father's mind was clear only for a moment. But this was one of those times which refused compromise. He didn't want to mention Peter out loud. He thought about her and Peter. Making love.

BEVERLEY SIMONS was born in Flin Flon in 1938, grew up in Edmonton, and settled in Vancouver in 1961. The author of such highly-acclaimed — if insufficiently-produced — plays as *Crabdance* and *Leela Means To Play*, the West Vancouver resident has also been involved in the creation of fiction in recent years. This has included several stories and the long, continuing novel from which we present an excerpt.

BEVERLEY SIMONS

an excerpt from the novel Da Vinci's Light

Laura

It was raining. Nothing new in that, but the headlights of her small car, bouncing back at Laura from the shimmering screen, made her feel uneasy. Each time driving through a rainy dusk it was the same — a repeated first experience, familiar to her only as if recalled from a dream. It wasn't yet completely dark. The luminous moving sculptures at the side of the road could be gusts of wind playing with the downpour, shaping it, creating temporal chimeras for her nervous eyes to interpret; or they could be bodies, people as cold and damp as she, floating in the half-light between their other more solid spheres of existence.

"The Homeric shades of the underworld," she whispered aloud, amused at her fancy. Laura's mind was usually preoccupied with practical substantive thoughts: lists of tasks, plans of possible action; and because she was a practical woman, each item had its modulated double: a reasonable alternative with an alternative scenario waiting to be unfurled if it became necessary.

A low contour, heavier than the other phantoms and remaining stubbornly congealed, disengaged itself from the side of the road. She slowed for it: an old grizzled dog, Lab and Shepherd mix, she'd guess. His head erect, he seemed preoccupied, indifferent to the wind and rain as he crossed calmly in front of her. She was reminded of Arthur Haynes. A temporary transmigration? When she'd last come across the professor he'd been equally unresponsive to the weather and the dangers of traffic. Carlights skimmed quickly over his vacant kindly face. She knew at once it was him by her irritation: That familiar childlike repose! It was out of place and unearned, damn it, as it always had been. But she was irritated, too, by the thrust of concerned guilt that she'd felt rise up out of her belly. Reality must whisper, and with a polite English accent when possible, so as not to waken Arthur Haynes unexpectedly. Dutiful women like Laura had helped keep it so: Accomplices, all of them. No longer her responsibility, she had Saul to worry about. But she watched with less objectivity than she would have liked while he shambled ahead without pause, expecting that traffic would allow him to pass through, unharmed as Moses through the Red Sea.

As with most children and many adults, his trust protected him. It went further than trust: he was wilfully blind. He ignored what was unpleasant or irrelevant to him. If he refused to recognize it, it did not exist. If it did not exist, it could not wound. ''Poison unacknowledged turns to milk'', he had told Laura. Sheathed in sparkling invisible armour he continued to survive; but like eggshell or fine glass, his armour needed one crack only to make the man inside instantly vulnerable. It had haunted Laura that she might have caused his first doubt: or had that been her hope? No, she didn't feel vengeful toward him; she'd wronged him. Was he warm enough? Would he cross safely?

She hadn't stopped. He was no longer her responsibility. That marriage was long behind her. He might not even recognize her; Laura wasn't sure if she could deal with that. Nor would she have welcomed recognition. For a moment, it was the beams of her car that shone directly into his eyes. He hadn't known that, of course. The eyes remained blank; there'd been no response to either the vehicle or its occupant. She could tell that he was shaping phrases to fill the stack of clean white paper waiting for him at home next to his typewriter.

He'd been wearing his gray tweed coat; it was as much his pelt as was the flecked glistening bristle of the dog. She watched him disappear through the veils of fine rain — The professor in the form of a dog. Had it been him? She imagined him on hind legs addressing a class on metempsychosis, and she laughed aloud.

Ahead of her, projecting somewhat into the road: a high thick cluster of shadow, which she interpreted as a thrust of trees. It would be a knoll typical of West Vancouver's stubborn rural identity. The older citizens defended every creek bed, every gnarled stump against the city's hunger for development.

Branches swung in the unpredictable currents of the night wind, darker against the silver-gleam of the rain, which still glowed with refracted sunlight, the source now invisible behind Bowen Island. Laura drowsily admired the moving pattern: it was a living Japanese screen that Saul's friend, Hannah, — *her friend, too* — might have dreamed and then painted. "*Beware the woods of Dunsinane.*" *Portents are silly.* Saul used to believe in them. She must call Hannah; check on the children; bring over some baking for them.

Weight, dissolved in the moist night light, had become motion, incorporeal. *e equals mc squared*. Science class could be made bearable, but she wasn't qualified; she'd been asked to teach it, would prefer not to, must talk to Gilbert, he'd understand. He meant well, but he was pushing her too fast.

One of the shadows broke, suddenly reasserting its dimension of mass. With a wild movement — impossible — it split from its trunk and was hurled or hurled itself — larger than a branch, it was a boy — in front of her. Her wheels spun crazily as she veered. Her responses were slow, she'd let the soft rain enter her; she saw a face or imagined she had: on it an expression, not of fear, but of despair and hate, he snarled up at her like a wild creature. Automatic pressure on the gas pedal took her to the corner, the momentum carried her around it.

She pulled over in front of a small church. It was hidden in the dark, but she knew it was there. The sidewalk in front and its generous lawns were used in the summertime by local farmers trying to bypass the chainstores. Laura's students had parttime jobs filling and emptying the trucks. Hard now to imagine baskets of sunwarmed berries, the sticky sweet odour... Not of blood....

Who were they? She knew enough about teenage behaviour to feel uneasy; there was more to it than the averted danger of an accident. She was tired: Behind her a full day's load of teaching and counselling, then a curriculum meeting; but she made herself start the car again and circle back to Marine Drive, travelling slowly, her eyes alert for the twolegged forest. And she saw them: They hurriedly crossed the street, melted behind hedges or into lanes as her eyes swung toward them; or flat down, they dropped to disappear into thick wet grass. She guessed most had already gone. No point in calling after them; certainly none in a chase; she'd look ridiculous. No-one had been hurt. She'd hear about it at school tomorrow. If she were there....

* * * * *

He wasn't sure how it had happened, when, slip slip, reality had shed itself like a skin. Things in themselves remained, deeper darker denser, but the connective membrane, God's sacred curtain, was dissolved.

There is supposed to be a substance spewed from the pores of mediums when deep in trance, a kind of mucous out of which bodies from other planes of existence are materialized. Fading Saul had understood that the substance was energy, the paste of society's agreed upon reality. Surely the individual citizen's most valuable contribution and his first duty was to hold that reality together. Poor Saul.... He could no longer endow even the objects in his room with significance or relationship. It was odd, he considered, the term insane: outsane would be more appropriate.

* * * * *

If she hadn't been tired and unsure of what to expect at home, or maybe because she was tired and unsure of what to expect — because, not if — she might allow the watery indefinite landscape to permeate her, might release herself into it. She, too, could dissolve and disappear. Stupid thought, uncharacteristic of her.... In any case, she'd have no time to consider it. Her headlights had illuminated a familiar trudging figure, who, unlike the professor, she could not ignore or pretend not to recognize. Steven Johannsen, the fifteen-year-old son of her best friend: he was a brilliant troublesome brat who had taken advantage of his mother since he was an infant. Laura had tried unsuccessfully to like him; Steven knew it, it put her at his mercy. He continually tried to expose what she would have to deny.

She honked and stopped for him. He made no move toward her, so she reached over and opened the passenger door. After a brief hesitation, Steven climbed in. His hostile look added to the draught, as did the wafting dampness of his saturated clothes; the boy was in unpleasant harmony with his miserable appearance. *The ninth and eleventh chords as Saul had explained them. Wagner's self-indulgence. I disapprove of it. I disapprove of unnecessary dissonance. I disapprove of Steven. Laura, the schoolmarm; Laura, Miss Myrtle.*

Exploiting his poor coordination, which he'd inherited from his father, he pretended he wasn't able to do up the seat belt or lock the door; Laura pretended not to notice. The boy's pale wet face was spotted with adolescent acne, the eyes were exposed; Steven hadn't yet learned how to hood the raw self-doubt that made others look away from him, embarassed; but his tight mouth, which refused to give up its habitual expression of superiority and disdain, staunched, as it always did, Laura's natural impulse of sympathy. The boy was stubbornly unappealing. She must try to keep in mind that it wasn't his fault; not all of it. Likely she'd been unappealing as a teenager. The thought, however, did not alter her responses. She scolded herself: as an adult she should be able to control and direct them.

While swivelling the car around to drive him home, she realized that the growling creature in front of her headlights had been Steven. She tried to reach for compassion, at least as a professional. It displeased her to feel, instead, irritation rise in answer to Steven's accusing silence. He knew it would; she knew he knew. It was as if in Steven's eyes she were the villain of the night, not the crowd of ruffians she'd disturbed.

"Why is Norma such a tart?" he finally blurted; she assumed he said it to anger her.

"Your mother's a fine person. I don't know anyone more courageous." Damn! She'd engaged; he was nearly as skillful as Saul.

"Norma's weird." It was a flat statement, but intended as well, she now realized, to explain what she'd seen. She should have guessed. His peers had been using his mother as an excuse to torment him. Norma was odd, certainly by West Vancouver standards, but Steven added to his difficulties with his sarcastic tongue and his pitiful swagger. He didn't know how to choose propitious moments of combat: he was impatient, like Norma. Nor did he attempt to distinguish antagonist from ally, witness the present; Norma was no diplomat either. He was stuck in a perverse attitude of rebellion that merely caricatured what he was trying to escape; it made him doubly ridiculous in the eyes of his schoolmates.

That he wanted to reject his unusual family and its history was understandable. Norma was wild quarry in a pseudo-bucolic setting. She was a gilded gamecock — the male bird better denoted her challenging stance — she inadvertently flushed the hunter's instinct in her neighbours.

The municipality of West Vancouver had originally been a summer retreat for retired or coupon clipping Britishers, later joined by those who aspired to the same heritage and hoped by imitation to acquire it. There were other, earlier natives: the Squamish Indians had kept themselves reasonably contained on a reservation at the mouth of the Capilano River, where eventually they earned dividends from their tact. They leased their acreages for camp sites and trailer courts, and finally for shopping malls, needed to satisfy the growing neighbourhoods of middle-class filling the land that rolled from mountain foothills to Howe Sound, an inlet of the Pacific Ocean. The North Shore was being "tamed and developed". Rivers and streams were made to change course as property values soared. Tractors toppled fir and cedar trees one hundred feet high. Neighbourhoods were created for those who had "made" it, those who hoped to, those who pretended that they had, and those who were testing new wealth before they'd spring from the North Shore to Shaugnessy itself, now a pitifully fragmented image of its former establishment grandeur, yet still a symbol of quiet wealth and inherited respectability, as enduring as the British crown. West Vancouver, too, had its claim to genteel history: The British Properties formed a second "reservation". But in this case exclusiveness was chosen, not thrust upon it. It had once boasted written guarantees of ghetto purity. There had been covenants against Chinks, Kikes, Niggers, and Wops.... The covenants had been challenged; they were no longer appropriate. Money had endowed new generations with respectability, if not breeding. Like a beneficient grandmother unrolling an apron larded with hidden, stored sweets, the land-holding company continued to release acreages for sale. Speculators forced prices still higher, high enough to attract the latest burgeoning of wealth. Irresistible to those raised on instant coffee and Kraft dinners. Here was an instant "address": it announced one's bank standing more surely than flashing a bank book, which would have been crude.

A view over Lions Gate Bridge to the city's highrises, and at night, its sparkling lights that reminded one of New York or Hong Kong, came with the deal. It was a useful feature that could be qualitatively measured and compared, prices adjusted accordingly. But sadly, it couldn't be avoided by those who desired the address without the vista. A wealthy Iranian, afraid of heights, had solved the problem. His blankwalled Alhambra became a favourite landmark for Sunday drivers and sightseers who respectfully cruised the growing centres of economic and architectural accomplishment.

Children from these homes had been taught not to respect

unusual lifestyles, unless they produced enough money to justify eccentricity or were well camouflaged. Norma did not fit into either category, but it wouldn't have mattered if she'd not had children. She rented a dilapidated beach cottage in a decidedly unfashionable district. High class shacks, really, they dated from the turn of the century when wealthy Vancouverites travelled by ferry to the North Shore to holiday in the summer. At night, the uninsulated walls resonated with the pattering traffic of rats. Many of her immediate neighbours were elderly people who, like Norma, were antagonized and bewildered by the influx of real estate pushers and strident shoppers. In some of the smaller houses, even in the newer districts, there were families who publicly admitted to low income, but they were few. But it was at the schools that the economic levels mixed: Nervous children relieved their tensions, acquired from anxious aggressive parents, by grouping to attack. The natural herd and heirarchy instinct was unnaturally sharpened. Steven and his sister, Justine, had been obvious quarry: children of a strange creature who perversely prided herself on being an oddball, they spoke in unusual rhythms and innocently applied a rich vocabulary acquired from their mother's books and from her friends; they had little in common with their peers. Norma was indifferent to the effect her dress and style of behaviour had on others; her children had not learned from her how to camouflage.

"I used to stand up for her, you know." Without prompting, Steven had begun to speak. "I was a fool, I know it now. I hate her — I know you think I'm like her, but I'm not." But he was still in awe of her, and he couldn't help being drawn into her irrepressible spicy conversation, which is why his attacks on her had grown more violent. He hated Norma for making him different, yet not different enough. He was too like another one already living, too much like her. He was neither accepted as one of his schoolmates nor was he unique. He was nothing at all.

When he showed symptoms of schizophrenia, Norma had

dutifully trooped him through an ever extending list of psychologists and psychiatrists, but he defied each of them to "name his gig". It was Laura's suspicion that he secretly read Norma's texts and aped the cases. She understood that Steven didn't like himself, that he'd found secondary comfort in recreating himself as he fancied — a mystery to the rest of the world — but it was the size of his gesture that made her impatient; and it pained her to watch Norma suffer from her brilliant baby's insults. She'd given up too much to raise the children.

Turning down Bellevue Avenue, Laura pulled into the driveway, and did a U-turn at the bottom. She could think of nothing to say to the hostile teenager who sulked next to her, blindly watching the rain roll down his window. A mock-up of professional support wouldn't do: he'd been well trained by Norma and he was sensitive, she had to give him that. She tried to smile to cover her aversion. If he picked it up, it would fuel his selfrighteous tendency to be cruel; Norma would get the brunt of it. *Smile, damn it*. Why couldn't she? It was Saul, that was it, she had nothing left to give; she had her own poison, her own household adolescent. He'd be waiting for her. *En garde*.

"Goodbye, Auntie Laura," Steven simpered in a dangerously meek tone; she knew there would be more. "Next time, piss off, will you?" He was standing outside, but he made no move to leave; he held the door firmly open. She started the car and pulled forward, Steven would look after himself. He jumped to the side onto the grass. She guessed he slid on a rotting apple, because she heard him curse, or thought she did, and, yes, the thud of its pulp against the back window....

"Let them kill me next time if that's what they want. What would you care anyway?" he shouted after her. She hoped the flapping door wouldn't catch on the narrow driveway gate. "It would give my mother and you more time to gossip." The voice was coming closer. "She wouldn't have to worry about me anymore." It was a sharp left onto Bellevue Avenue. He was just behind her now, he must be running. The passenger door swung itself shut, but she could still hear him: "Norma could fuck whenever she wanted to...." She knew the subtext of the foul language was entreaty, but she'd have preferred not to have heard either.

* * * * *

D. M. FRASER was born in Nova Scotia in 1946 and died March, 1985, in Vancouver. He was educated at Acadia University and U.B.C. His critically acclaimed novels include *Class Warfare* (1974) and *The Voice Of Emma Sachs* (1983). His premature loss is sorely lamented.

D.M. FRASER

for Snipe, to remember us by

Recessional

The noise would have been deafening, if we'd had ears to hear. The Vancouverites came out of the woodwork like fruit-flies on sabbatical; they sang and danced and clapped their paws; they embraced one another warmly, coldly, temperately, as befits refugees from the Temperate Zone. They carried their history, jealously, in brand-name shopping bags, and they wore their hearts on their running shoes. The males all wore shorts that looked like underwear; the leaders among them had base-ball caps to disguise their bald spots. The females had mesh halters and hairy legs: that was how we could tell the difference. "We must love one another or die," Augustine said. I said, "You don't leave a guy much choice in the matter, do you?" This sort of exchange is what passes for conversation with the Vancouverites. When not engaged in profundities, they merely grind their dentures and hum. In their sleep, they chew the ends of pencils.

We apologize for the randomness of this report, for infelicities of observation and diction, for personal stains on the paper. Everything was falling apart, and we alone seemed to notice. Is it any wonder we left early, before the general collapse became particular? We tried our damndest to do things right, according to the laws of Vancouverites, but all the things we did were damned from the start. We won the Dream Home, for instance, and lost it as soon as we imagined ourselves living in it. All those appliances! Gone forever! We put a curse on the Dream Home, but we doubt it will have any effect. The Vancouverites aren't interested in curses; they're emigrating to Saskatoon.

"I love you," Augustine said as we were extricating ourselves from the Horticulture Show. This is a kind of prayer the

Vancouverites make a point of saying at least once a day, as other peoples, more primitive and less desperate, mumble incantations over their potato salad. The correct response, as yet unlearned by God, is, "I love you, too." Striving toward correctitude, I said to Augustine, "I loved you, too." He said, after the fashion of the Vancouverites, "How much money do you have?"

When I woke, I was astonished to find you there, alive and snoring beside me, looking as though you belonged where you were.

We found these words, written on a napkin, among various embarrassments left behind in the early confusions of the exodus. It must have been part of a letter someone was attempting to write to someone else, the letter that night have gone on to remark, *I need you all the time, don't leave me, don't change, don't die.* Such humble requests are put in writing frequently, hereabouts, and we understand that nobody is required to take them seriously. The capability of desire is its own fulfillment; the rest is spray-painting. "Loving you," Augustine said, "is carrying coals to Newcastle." That struck me as a dangerously Vancouveritical thing to say: only rubbies, bag ladies and professors of English would stand a chance of understanding it, and I take it as a slur on my hygeine. At the time, I took it as a joke.

Dear Mum: The mountains are beautiful. They go up and up and up into the sky, just like in the pictures Daddy brought back from Vancouver when he and Lucy ran away together. Why did they run away? Did they really run? With their feet? Did they run for Cancer? You don't have to answer if it'll hurt your feelings.

The water stays in harbour, where it belongs. It'd be blue if the sun ever shone. The mountains are crisscrossed with Dream Homes. Here, Augustine, is our song:

I'll find another shore, another sea.
A better city.
Everything I've done has gone astray;
My heart is dumped.
How long will I live in stucco heaven?
Everywhere I look
Black ruins face me
Here
Where I spent so long making a fool of me.

We apologize again. When the Vancouverites were leaving, they went to Greek restaurants; so did we, who found that poem on the flip side of a menu. "How long," Augustine said, "will I keep my nose up a barrel of leftovers?" I said, "What do you mean?" He said, "It's in the nature of our assignment not to tell the truth. We can love but we can't can't. The mountains go up to the sky and the water goes down to the bottom, but you and I stand on the blasted plain, swaying." There was a dreadful pause. We'd agreed that private sentiments, abstract erections and political opinions wouldn't enter into this report: someone's Serving Person might fall off the British Improprieties.

Dear Augie: This is my first try at saying good-bye to you. Forgive me if I revise it a few times before one of us kills me. I'm worried about something, but I don't want to write another sentence which has "but" following a comma, as if the world were reversible. "Tell me a story," you said. Can you imagine how furiously I wanted to? I didn't have any to offer. The Vancouverites were packing their bags. If we'd had ears, we'd have heard them in Thunder Bay, putting small things inside larger things, to carry away with them. What shall we, Augustine, carry away with us? Beautiful memories? Crabs? Gorgeous as it resembles, the sunset tonight bodes ill, and we have no small things left to put in large bags. All the Greek restaurants have closed. The trolleys sleep. Your face in repose is the brightest light in town. Help!

God, it takes a long time to write a memo. We have no wish to blame the Vancouverites, whose accomplishments include the fine art of memo-writing. "Can you accept the fall of civilization?" Augustine asked politely. "How can I not?" I replied bravely. We shared an instant of instant insight. Like mice inheriting a basement suite, thoughts scurried across our . . . minds. What colour were your eyes? How yellow your teeth? We only begged to know how those poor souls lived, what and why they ate, how they disported themselves under the blankets they left behind. Did they, like us, begin at the beginning and muddle back to the end? Did they enjoy life before they traded it in? We may never know. It's been said of these creatures that they often talk to themselves, seldom to one another. What, we wonder, do they construct to talk *about?*

Dear Nellie: I hate to mention this, but I think the world is ending. As you so wisely said, it has no right to do that without consulting us, but under Canadian law it has no right not to do it. We're already reduced to sentence structures of such loathesome simplicity that even you can comprehend them. I put your bra and panties in the fridge, to warm them up for you.

It bothered us that, having been instructed not to pity them, we found every other available emotion unsuitable. Tenderness was out of the question. Rage was laughable. Hatred is, as you're aware, no respecter of persons, and respect of persons was implicit in our orders. Tolerance is boring. We had no trouble infiltrating the Vancouverites, who so nearly resemble us that none of them perceived our strangeness in their midst; yet we are having extraordinary trouble getting away from them. They cling to us when we go to the bathroom, they follow us to the laundromat, they read our letters and bank statements, they advise us on the disposition of our disposition. They are no respecters of tenses: what is past is present to them, and everything is going to happen last year.

Dear Jim: By the time you read this I won't be dead. Sorry. The pizza was great. Love, Betty Lou.

Before the exodus, the orthodox Vancouverites went to the park to pay a last homage. They went on bicycles and in push-carts, they went in jeans and tanktops, they went in droves, they went naked. Their artists had arranged an exhibition of pretty pictures, mostly of mountains, so they'd have something to take away with them if they wanted to. It was touching how few wanted to. "This is touching," Augustine said, "don't you think?" I said: "Hardly ever." It occurred to us that touching is something the Vancouverites did a lot of, in their prime, without looking at what they touched, so that their fingers dropped off. You can retrieve them in Kitsilano, we're told, licking themselves in a health-food restaurant. Frankly, we're at a loss for words. Where is Kitsilano? What is a health food? When is the meaning of life?

Dear John: Now that you've left I wish you hadn't. It would have been nice to see your smiling face across our hangover tomorrow. I'm hearing sirens, but they ain't the type that lean out of windows or perch on rocks in them classical poems you read all the time. The sky is orange. I see no reason why, aesthetically speaking, the sky shouldn't have the liberty to choose its colour, but we might have talked it over. There are whole piles of things we might have talked over, if the sky could talk. John, come back. The sky is a deeper orange than it used to be. This situation is expanding. I am not. Unfortunately, I have one of your socks on my left foot, the blue one — wait a minute, the sock's the foot that's blue — Oh Lord, the brown sock's on your right foot, I don't know what you move so fast for. Stay still. The sky's a lovely shade of purple, a vast improvement on orange. Do you think they cared?

Without ears, we nonetheless aim toward coherence. More often than not, we miss. Everywhere we turned our burned-out eyes, the Vancouverites were achieving coherence: they were leaving town. Aim toward coherence, they recommended. Leave town, they whispered. Their little voices drifted in the wind; the wind drifted in the window; nothing made sense. If we'd had ears to hear, it could have been a different story.Augustine would have turned his large and sleepy shoulders, and mashed my mouth. Instead, he said, "What the hell are we gonna tell them?" I said: "Anything." He said: "I've never been to Saskatoon." I said: "Invent it. If it's good enough for the Vancouverites it's bad enough for you." We hold each other, and there wasn't a drop of coherence on the horizon. "Enough's enough," Augustine said, as I thought how smart he was to say it before I thought of it.

Dear Claire: You may have wondered why my buddy Augustine and I sit at your feet every night. I would now like to explain this awkward circumstance for which, let me assure you, my buddy Augustine would join me in making, if he could, excuses. We came here to study the Vancouverites, but we got tired of them. And, *just for the record, we got tired of them. You, however, have terrific feet, which Augie and me is content to sit at the soul of. I spelled that wrong and I decline to correct it; grown bigger ears, I hear music everywhere I travel, everywhere I roam. Your job is to sing it. From your podium, you can't see us weep, you can't be allowed to weep. We do it for you. Do you, for a moment of your wakened life, suppose that we want the pizza, the Secreat Special? We don't. Your feet in my hair is, are, would be, possibly might have been, sufficient. "Do you love me?" Augustine said. "Oh for Their sake," I said, "could you ask me something new?"* The beginning iv. The Vancouverites are panickinh. *I can't spell anything. You have great feet.*

Let us forgive them. The documents they left us indicate that they were adaptable to affection, and not usually hostile to the likes of us. They had large arms to slump around us, and tiny ears to hear us when we fell. They didn't smell too bad.

They were tough trees to lean on when the wind was wrong. When they went missing, the words they left behind were peace of mind. We've copied as many as we could gather? Claire? John? Jim? What did they want? That's the smart question Augie answered: me. Of course.

Dear Tom: I want to hear you play your guitar. Confusions confound us, as we go away, as we strive toward towardness? Please love me. When the Vancouverites took off, they didn't leave any signs. Let us remember them,,,,. There were only glances that we missed. Nothing worked. Jim, I want to tell you one last story, and I promise it won't have plot or answer; they were leaving fast, there wasn't time, grow bigger ears, the Vancouverites are
Claire I can't spell your name can you . . . ?
on the loose. Look, we shouldn't talk about this. What have you got invested in which tower? Rehab City?

What do you think it meant by that?

The sky is now invisible. Can we start from scratch?

Gibble them time to enjoy themselves. Gibble them time to wipe the snot off their faces. Their faces were beautiful. We concluded that the Vancouverites, for all their manifest flaws, were beautiful in their way, and ought to have been allowed to continue the practice of beauty. We discovered, to our enduring shame, that we loved them as they were.

Fifty year-old, Binghamton, N.Y. born AUDREY THOMAS has been associated with Vancouver since the late 1950s. Her ten published volumes of fiction include *Mrs. Blood, Munchmeyer* and *Prospero On The Island*, and her most recent novel, *Intertidal Life*. She has just completed a new volume of stories, *Good-bye, Harold, Good Luck*.

AUDREY THOMAS

Trash

My husband always used to let me choose the tenants for the upstairs suite. Perhaps "let" isn't exactly the right word as I was perfectly aware of the fact that he didn't want anything to do with it — the choosing of tenants — if he could possibly avoid it. That way it was clear from the beginning that I was the landlady and the rules — no typing after 11 p.m., no baths or showers before 6 a.m., no rowdy parties, rent due and payable on the last day of each month — were *my* rules, nothing to do with him. He was just the pleasant if somewhat distant husband of the landlady, the man who said "hello" or "hello there" in passing and changed a fuse if a circuit got overloaded.

"You'll see to it, won't you," he would say as the time drew near for our annual ad in the university rental sheet. "You see to it, won't you? You do it so well." His contribution was cleaning up after the last tenants (another rule was "please leave this suite the way you found it" but nobody ever did and this was the early sixties, long before the days of damage deposits and the many regulations that now make up the Landlord and Tenant Act). He mended any of the Sally Ann furniture that needed mending or replaced it with more of the same if it was beyond repair. He washed the walls and painted them if they were too grimy. So he did his share, no doubt about that, but I was always the one who had to deal with the actual people.

We never rented out the upstairs suite for more than ten months: during July and August relatives visited, or friends, and it was nice to have a place to put them where they (and we) could have some privacy. Ours was an old house, just south of Broadway, near Alma, in a shabby genteel district. Not a very interesting house architecturally but large and friendly and from the bathroom in the upstairs suite you got a view of the mountains. The suite was very easy to rent out.

And so, along about the middle of August our name would go in to the University, the telephone would start ringing and I would interview prospective tenants, traipse them up and down the stairs, show them the rules which I had typed neatly and posted on the back of the door — like the rules in a French hotel or pension — and if we all liked each other well enough to enter into a relationship of this sort, they would sign another copy of the rules, give me the first and last months rent in advance and move in the end of the month.

I had to be strict. I too was a student, doing graduate work, and we had two young children. I studied at night, after the kids were in bed, and for two hours in the early mornings, before everybody woke up. I was also a TA (a teaching assistant) in order to get the money for my fees and a baby-sitter the few hours a week I was actually teaching or in a Seminar. I never stayed at the University to study and my social life up there was limited to a coffee at the Graduate Centre if I had an hour between classes. One of the male graduate students once told me he thought I was a very "Romantic" figure, the way I kept appearing and disappearing so mysteriously. I just looked at him.

So I studied in the kitchen, sometimes falling asleep right there with my head on a book or a pile of English 100 essays. My husband would eventually miss me and come wake me up, insisting I go to bed. When I think back on those years now I see myself as always tired and grumpy but neither my friends nor my children remember me that way at all. I must have been a better actress than I thought. I seemed to see the world through a glassy shimmer, the way you see the landscape near a barbeque or campfire.

We had a basement suite as well but that was more or less permanently rented to a tugboat captain who worked for Kingcome Navigation and was away more than he was at home. He had a separate entrance (the real drawback with the upstairs suite was that it shared the same entrance as we had) and we hardly ever saw him except once in a while along Broadway, always wearing a grey felt hat. Once he bought the children ice-cream cones when we happened to meet in *Peter's.* He used to get a newspaper from the John Howard Society (one of my other duties as landlady was to sort out all the mail and deliver it to the tenants or forward it if they'd moved on) and I never even glanced at it, never knew what it was until one Christmas afternoon, just as we were about to carve the turkey in front of an admiring group of students from International House, Cap'n Willis staggered up the backporch stairs and asked my husband to take him to the hospital. He'd been on a three day bender, drinking vodka and eating nothing and was seeing things. I was fascinated by the fact that sick as he was (and he was a terrible colour) he was wearing his grey felt hat. After a few weeks he reappeared, apoligized and vowed it would never happen again. He was with us for another year quiet as could be, and then he took a job up in Prince Rupert. The John Howard Society newsletter came for years (it was the only mail he ever got) but he'd left no forwarding address so I just threw it away.

So, except for that one solitary incident the basement suite had never been a problem but the upstairs suite was another matter altogether. For one thing, it usually involved two people living directly over our heads (one year two Japanese-Canadian sisters, another year a young Canadian in the German department and his new German wife, once two young men from the Vancouver School of Art) and, as I have already mentioned, there was no separate entrance for this suite. We had French doors on the sitting-room (to the left as you came in) and a door on the childrens' room (to the right) but tenants had to come up the front steps, open the front door and proceed up the stairs to the suite. All this never seemed to bother them but it bothered me. It *really* bothered me. Our house was old and had no insulation whatsoever; every noise carried. I could hardly legislate what time people came in (it had occurred to me to put in the rules "no admittance after 11 p.m." but I knew I couldn't do that, it wouldn't be fair) and so I put up with people knocking over the milkbottles which had been carefully put out for the Dairyland man or calling cheerful, loud good-byes to friends who had dropped them off. The kids woke up and as I was in the kitchen I was the one who went to comfort them: "Shh, shh, it's only John and Trudl, Joe and Simon, Hannah and Allan, shh, shh."

And so our life continued, me studying on the kitchen table, the children growing a little older — one of them now at the Acadia Daycare Centre three mornings a week, an amazing thing for me as daycare was not yet an accepted thing — my husband continuing to ask me to choose the tenants "because you do it so well." I was longing for a study, a room of my own, tired of always having to remove my books from the kitchen table while I cooked or we ate or played games with the children. We had no dining-room; we slept in what had been the dining-room. The shimmering haze through which I viewed the world seemed to be getting worse. I had completed my MA thesis — god knows how — and was studying for my comprehensives. I was also teaching two sections of English 100 and exams were coming up. I was trying to be Super-Mother, never a TV dinner in our house or a cake mix. People said "I don't know how you do it." I should have paid attention to such remarks but of course I didn't. I was flattered and determined to try harder. But I began to resent my husband's attitude to all this. I kept asking him when when *when* can we stop renting out one of the suites, when can I have a place, a study, a corner for myself? He said soon, soon (in the same tone I used to hush the children, "shh, shh") we can't quite afford it just yet.

And then we decided to go to England for the summer, to see my husband's parents. There was some terrific fare available through the BC Teachers' Federation and as our youngest was not quite two, she could go free. Our eldest was born in England but the grandparents had never seen the little one. It was too good an opportunity to pass up. I was to take my comprehensives in June and we would be away for July and August. (I wanted to say to him why don't you leave me here and take the children on your own but I couldn't think of a valid reason. My teaching would be over, my comprehensives — presumably — passed. There was no excuse for staying behind. I couldn't bring myself to say "I want to be alone, I want to *stop* for a while." For when, really, did he stop, when did he have a spell of time to call *his* own? Besides, we would need to rent out the house to help towards the cost of the trip.) Deep down I was seething with resentment. The money for the trip would have paid for the upstairs suite to be empty for at least six months. A room — *rooms* — to work in, study in, be alone in. For I was a glutton for punishment; I had enrolled as a candidate for a PhD. And I wanted to spend a summer camping, or sprawled in our own backyard. Vancouver was lovely in the summertime, still is. Why go to England and dress up the children and be polite? But I agreed to it all and even began making little summer dresses and telling stories about England, about Grannie and Grandpa, instead of the usual bedtime stories. And I knew how much my husband's parents missed him; they hadn't seen him in five years.

A teacher from Golden, BC, arranged to take the entire house — except the basement suite — for July and August. I was pleased that was settled so easily and I could get on with my studying. Our most recent tenant had left a few weeks before the end of April. He was a nice young man whose girlfriend slept over on the weekends. The two of them made, boisterous love directly over our sitting-room every Saturday night. We got used to it, more or less, but it was pretty awful if we had guests. We would all raise our voices as things got more and more vocal until we were practically shouting at one another, and then gradually sink back into normal conversation as the cries diminished to moans and sighs. My husband wanted me to speak to him, discreetly, but there I drew the line. "Speak to him yourself" I said, but he never did. Sunday mornings I would see them go off hand in hand to catch the bus to her place, where they spent Sunday nights. He was a graduate student in biology — something to do with the brains of hummingbirds.

Over dinner one night in early May my husband suggested we rent out the upstairs suite for six weeks, at a reduced rate — it would be a little extra cash for the trip. We had a terrific row about that — I had moved my books to the upstairs kitchen — but somehow he persuaded me, he always could. We would leave the children with his parents and have a slap-up weekend in London on our own — something like that. I went and retrieved my books and papers and brought them all downstairs. Then I placed an ad in the *Sun* for three days and waited. Who would want a suite for only six weeks? I hoped no one would answer and on the first day no one did. The second day several people came but either they wanted to negotiate a longer rental or I didn't like their looks and quickly thought of new rules (no smoking, no overnight visitors). In one instance I told the people that we were vegetarians and couldn't possibly rent to anyone who cooked meat. I was shameless that day in my attempts to keep the suite for myself.

And then, around 4:30 in the afternoon a young couple with a baby knocked on the door. The ad said "no children, no pets" so I was very surprised. I asked them if they had read the ad carefully and they said yes, but they'd driven all the way from Calgary and were desperate for a place to stay. Just for six weeks. They had a cousin in Burnaby who had promised they could move in with her on July 1st. The husband — Danny — had been offered a temporary job as an emcee in a nightclub downtown. He was "in the entertainment business" but this was the first work he'd found in months. So they'd packed up and driven all night, but hadn't known how hard it would be to find a place that would take a baby.

They were very young, maybe 19 (the girl) and 20 (the boy). I wasn't much older myself, 26, but I *felt* older, a woman who had a husband with a steady job, a house with suites, two clean, well-fed children who didn't have to be packed up and driven through the mountains to another city because their father couldn't find a job. I might bitch about lack of space and too much to do but really I had had a pretty nice life so far. I tell you all this because I am trying to explain why, after all my lies and manoeuvres to keep out several prospective tenants who would probably be much more congenial, more reliable, than this bedraggled pair and their baby, I decided to rent to them. Once inside (and after they'd seen the upstairs) the girl kept looking around our sittingroom and saying "This is sure nice" and smiling at my daughters, who were intrigued by the baby, a sickly-looking boy of about nine months. I felt *guilty.* I knew it was madness, that I was already operating on a kind of emotional overdraft and that I would probably regret it the next day, but I rented to them. I did insist on cash, not a cheque, and a month's rent in advance. When the young man, who was a bit of a swaggerer and darkly good-looking in a sharp-faced way, mentioned again that he'd be working nights, I got him to promise to wear running shoes going to and from his job. Then I lent them our old crib, a playpen, coffee, milk, sugar and left them to settle in. The suite had been freshly painted and I had put a jug of spring flowers on the kitchen table. "Oh," the girl said to me, "I just know our luck's gonna change in a place like this."

Need I say that my husband thought I'd gone off my head, that we had a strict rule about no children and for a very good reason. I'd have to go up there and tell them there'd been some mistake. "You go," I said, "You tell them." And then, basking in the warm glow of a Good Deed I added "We have *so much!*"

"Well," he said, "it's up to you of course; you're the one with exams coming up. I just hope you don't regret it."

And it was all right for the first ten days or so. The girl, Margie, was the one I saw most. I let her use our washing machine and she came down every other day with a load of soiled clothes, mostly baby clothes, and washed them while the baby had his nap, or put him on a blanket in the garden if he were awake. She had her own clothes pegs with her, the ends marked with bright red nail polish so her pegs wouldn't get mixed up with mine. She was a pale, long-legged girl, taller than her husband, with frizzy brown hair. If the weather were nice she sometimes sat in the backyard and read a movie magazine while the clothes were doing. She told me the baby's name was Kojack because she'd been watching that programme when her pains began and besides she thought Telly Savalas was really sexy. She was surprised that we didn't have a TV and didn't allow one in the suite. She said they sold their TV and all their furniture before they left Calgary but it was the first thing they were going to buy when they got some money together. But she seemed to be a good mother, quite content to look after the baby while her husband slept most of the day away — he was out of the house from 10 p.m. to 8 a.m. every day except Sunday. He'd sold the car the day after they arrived but I'd sometimes see them together in the late afternoon, taking the baby for a walk before dinner. She didn't cook much, or at least very few cooking smells came from the upstairs suite and the delivery boy from Boston Pizza showed up a lot at the front door. Danny had certainly kept his word about being quiet — we never heard him go out at night unless we happened to be reading in the sitting-room.

And then one night there was the sound of a TV upstairs, quite loud. I mentioned this to Margie the next day and she turned quite sulky. She was bored at night, she said, with nothing to do and nowhere to go. Danny had borrowed it from one of the fellows at the club. It was company. I explained once again about my exams. She said she'd keep it down. I said no, I didn't want the TV at all and Danny would have to give it back. She gave me a funny smile and shrugged.

"You're the boss."

"That's right," I said, "I am." And tried not to feel guilty at the thought of her upstairs, unable to sleep, unable, even, to go out for a late-night walk because of the sleeping baby. I offered to listen for the baby if she wanted to go out for an hour or so some night.

"Where to?" she said.

"Just for a walk. It's a nice neighbourhood to walk in."

"*Is* it?" she said and smiled that funny smile again.

That night it appeared that Danny hadn't gone to work for we heard the sounds of an argument, low, continuous, furious, long after he usually left the house. The next night there was more argument and then the sound of somebody hammering something to the upstairs door. My husband looked at me as much to say, "it's your problem, you wanted them here," so I went up the stairs and knocked. No answer. I knocked again, louder. Finally a bolt slid back and the door opened a little way. It was held in place by a chain. Margie's face appeared in the crack.

"Oh," she said with a certain relief, "It's you."

"I was wondering about the hammering," I said, "but now I see you were putting on a bolt and chain. You should have asked me before you did that you know. The front door is locked at night; you're perfectly safe."

She just stared at me, a small defiant smile on her face. She said what she had obviously rehearsed.

"We're entitled to some privacy."

"No one is interfering with your privacy in any way," I said. "We've never had a lock on that door because this is an old house and there is no fire escape. However, we would never go up except in an emergency. How would we get to you quickly if the door was locked?"

"There isn't gonna be no emergency," she said, and shut the door in my face.

I went back downstairs and asked my husband what to do.

"Leave it," he said, "we'll remove it when they've gone."

"It's pretty weird," I said. "I think she was expecting someone else to knock on the door, but who? Nobody could get past the front door at night unless they had a key. Do you suppose they've run up some huge debts and are afraid of bill collectors?''

''In two weeks?''

''Maybe in Calgary before they came?''

He smiled. ''Just get on with your studying.''

I figured they were in some kind of trouble but tried not to think about it — there were only three more weeks until my exams. But the next night, just as I was removing my books and cards from the kitchen table, I heard a strange noise in the childrens' room (it was very late, maybe 2 a.m.) and went down the hall to see what it was. A strange man was just shutting the door to the childrens' room. I was so angry I forgot to be afraid.

''Who are you! What are you doing here!''

''I live here,'' he said quietly, and went quickly up the stairs to the suite. As I stood at the bottom, my heart pounding, he unlocked the door and went in, drawing the bolt in place as soon as he'd closed the door.

After checking that the children were all right I woke my husband.

''Maybe he's a friend of theirs, just spending the night.''

''He said he *lived* here! And the way he said it. Please go and see what's going on, *please.* He was just standing there outside the childrens' room. I think he'd been in there or was about to go in. I'm *afraid.*''

At that my husband put on his dressing gown and went to investigate. I heard him knock softly, no answer, knock again and again. No one came to the door. He went up again in the morning before work, but there was still no answer.

''Well they can't stay in there forever,'' he said. ''No doubt Margie will come down to do the baby's things and you can ask her what it's all about.''

That's when I realized she hadn't been down to do the wash in several days. In fact, I hadn't seen anything of her except for her face at the crack of the upstairs door.

''I think we should call the police,'' I said.

''Oh come. The man you saw was probably just a friend

staying the night who couldn't remember where the stairs were."

"The stairs are right there, as soon as you open the front door!"

"Well maybe he was a bit drunk. Why don't you take a day off and go to the beach with the kids, you've been working too hard."

I resented the implications of that remark but I did go to the beach. I didn't feel like staying in the house alone. I called a friend and she and I and our kids all went for a picnic at Spanish Banks. Afterwards she came back with me and stood at the bottom of the stairs while I went up and knocked, no pounded, on the upstairs door.

"I really don't like this," I said to my girlfriend. "I'm going to call the police."

"Police, police!" shouted all the kids, very excited. "She's going to call the police!"

At that minute the bolt shot back and Margie, white-faced, anxious, peered out at me.

"Whadya want? You woke the baby up. Why don't you leave us alone?"

"I want to come in for a minute. I want some explanations." I could hear the baby wailing in the other room and the TV turned down low.

"I haven't done nothing," she said, "you're the ones who are always banging on the door."

"I was very frightened to find a strange man in the house last night," I said. "He had a key to the front door and to your door and he said he lives here."

She looked at me, holding her cotton robe together with her free hand, ready to slam the door shut with the other if I should try to force my way in.

"So?" she said.

"So why didn't you tell me you'd invited somebody else to stay with you. You can't do that. We never have more than two people in this suite. I already made an exception for your baby."

"Aren't you wonderful," she said softly, and then "it's okay, there's only two people here."

"What do you mean? That man said he lived here." (I heard my voice saying "that man".)

"That man's name is Fred and he does live here."

"Where's Danny?"

"Gone," she said, and slammed the door.

"I'm calling the police," I shouted through the door, "right now."

I raced downstairs like a madwoman, shouted "don't go!" to my friend and dialed the police. After a bit of explanation I was transferred to the dective in charge of the Boarding House Detail. Sounds like something out of an old radio play, doesn't it, but I assure you it exists, or did in Vancouver in 1963. I can't remember the man's name but he listened patiently for a while and then he broke in to ask me what these people looked like. I described them, sharp-faced Danny, tall, thin Margie and her baby and the Mystery Man. He laughed.

"You sure got yourself mixed up with some lulus," he said, "and there isn't an awful lot I can do about it."

"You *know* these people?"

"I know all of them. Danny and Margie, *not* their real names by the way, are just chicken-shit, if you'll pardon my French —"

"Chicken-shit?"

"Petty thievery, the occasional stolen car, nothing dangerous. I didn't know about the kid. But the other guy — he's not so nice. I wouldn't turn my back on the other guy. If he's who I think he is and he sure sounds like it."

"Can't you come down and arrest them right now?"

"No. There's very little I can do. None of them are wanted for anything — at the minute." He laughed. "They sure sold you a bill of goods."

"I'm scared," I said. "I've got two kids, my husband's away all day and I'm scared."

"Is the third man up there right now?"

"I don't know — I've been at the beach all day. Margie's up there with the baby, that's all I know."

He thought a minute. "Tell her that I want to talk to her." And he gave his name.

"She won't come down."

"I think she will."

And she did, locking the upstairs behind her, still in the cotton robe. I handed her the phone and went out of the kitchen and into the sitting-room where my girlfriend was trying to keep all the kids amused.

"What's happening?" she said.

"I'm not sure yet."

"Are the police coming?" said the kids.

Margie stuck her head in the sitting-room door. "He wants to talk to *you*," she said. "It's okay, we're clearing out but we want our money back." She gave me such a look of exhausted hate that I've never forgotten it.

I went back into the kitchen and picked up the phone.

"She's going to leave" the detective said, "And the man Fred is out at the minute. You have every legal right to refuse him entry. Go and bolt your front door and just let Margie out or in. According to her, things were getting a bit uncomfortable and Danny's long gone, he won't trouble you. But do me a favour and change your locks just the same. You'll have to give her back the rent."

"I don't care," I said, and then, "what did you say to her?"

"Never mind. That's between Margie and me." He paused. "I'd like you to do me another favour."

"What's that."

"You sound like an intelligent woman and I'm sure you have a warm heart. But the next time you rent to a stranger, even if she looks like your little old grannie, call me and give me a description? What I've done to-day — well, I might not be able to do it again. Fred is not nice, not nice at all."

I wrote down his name and number, thanked him and hung up. Margie had gotten dressed and was dragging stuff down the stairs and onto the porch. When everything was out there she went and got the baby and muttered something about going off to the payphone on the corner of Broadway to call a friend. I locked and bolted the door behind her in case Fred came back.

Then I realized she had left the upstairs wide open and I went up, not really out of curiosity but to make sure that she hadn't left anything behind. I couldn't believe what I saw. The TV's, tape recorders, things like that didn't bother me. I'd sort of expected that after talking to the detective. But the floors were filthy, covered in chewing gum, food wrappers, used condoms, spilled pop. The kitchen table had a huge burn where a hot frying pan had been set down on top of it and the whole place stank from a huge pail of dirty diapers. She had even taken a dirty diaper and rubbed it hard across the kitchen walls.

I stood there, trying to catch my breath. And then I went and stood by the front door, which was glass-panelled, and watched her sitting on the porch railing, smoking, the baby in her arms, waiting for her ride. And when her "friend" showed up — it could have been her older sister or her mother, there was a strong family resemblance — I stepped out onto the porch and did something I've always been ashamed of. I shouted at her, as loud as I could, so the whole neighbourhood could hear, "You're trash, that's what you are, just trash!"

Then I went back inside and slammed the door and locked it.

KEATH FRASER is the 40 year-old author of the volume of short stories, *Taking Cover* (1982). Another collection, *Foreign Affairs*, is due from General this fall. Dr. Fraser's background is academic. A Ph.D. from the University of London led to a five-year stint in the English Department at the University of Calgary. He now lives in Vancouver, working as a free-lance writer and critic.

KEATH FRASER

There Are More Dark Women In The World Than Light

That spring he began calling on her often enough to leave his lock and chain wrapped around the Japanese cherry tree by her building. He saw no point in carrying the chain home every night. He would pedal home and park behind his Toyota Celica in the locked underground garage. Then in June she went away on holidays to visit relatives in Utrecht. She didn't *want* to go, she said leaving the West Coast in June was like eating curry for Christmas. "You know, Sad City." When she returned he pumped over and discovered his lock and chain had disappeared.

"Well, Dimwit, you'll have to park in the lobby from now on." She said the interesting thing about the Netherlands was how *many* people rode bicycles. "With wicker baskets, full of cheese wheels and glads." In Amsterdam she saw Anne Frank's house again, the Red Light District, and far too many twenty-course Indonesian reistafels. He could see she had put on weight. She bemoaned her trip because of what had happened to her forehand since going away. And over coffee she made him open his present. "It's not anything great," she told him. A lavender candle, he discovered, shaped like a phallus. "They're for sale all over the Rembrandtsplein," she explained. He lit it, with a smile, and before it burned halfway down they'd made a homecoming of love. The candle cast a guttering, mellow light at dusk. Except its smoke got in their eyes, and she licked her thumb and forefinger to snuff the flame. The lustre slid from her eyes and her hair came down in ringlets. If only she didn't have to go back to work until at least her tennis improved, she murmured. She disliked the Trust Company and was thinking of going over to a real bank. "You know, an old-fashioned one with marble columns and chandeliers?'' She wondered how many of those institutions were left.

He took his own holidays in August, though he would have preferred October, and went fishing in Ontario. The acid rain in the lake had killed all the fish. He was surprised and told his brother they should think of selling the family cottage. His brother, who had black spots in his nails from banging up wallboard, said no one wanted to buy into a dead lake. He should have warned him to stay in Toronto. Anyway, it was still an okay lake for water-skiing and reading books, but if he wanted trout fishing to try Algonquin Park.

Instead he flew to San Francisco. Casting around in bars for a little action, he got off a few good lines with a young woman in pearls, who told him she was engaged to a financier in Connecticut. ''Wants to retire by the time he's forty,'' she said. Adding, ''I don't really know why I come here, I know all these people.'' From her office, she meant, but standing there with a Heineken in hand she wasn't talking to anyone he'd noticed. They shared a few laughs, she liked Sissy Spacek and he didn't, and then she left, taking along her dry-cleaning in cellophane from the coat rack. The bar was crowded and loud. A young Vietnamese with nobody to talk to said hi. He was in marine insurance, finishing a college degree at night in business administration, about which he wasn't sanguine. ''People tell me to count on future,'' he said. ''Now is first time in history population of San Francisco is not mainly Caucasian.'' He dropped his articles and drank pernod, looking uneasy among these lawyers and brokers. The bar was on Union Street.

In October he bought another lock and chain to bind his ten-speed Norco to the cherry tree. As before, he left the chain behind in the grass when he rode home at night. He really only used the bike to ride to her place, or occasionally around the park. But driving home from work one afternoon he noticed someone had stolen his bike from the garage. Luckily it was December then and raining every day, so what he didn't much ride he never really missed. In fact he rarely thought of cycling till the warm March sun returned, and he felt his legs could have done with a good pump. The police never phoned him back.

By this time he had known her a year and a half. She was still with the Trust Company and wondering now if they shouldn't take their holidays together. Trouble was she had August, and he October. He told her if she had come up with her bright idea last January they might have co-ordinated their plans. "You sound just as happy I didn't," she said. Anyhow, it didn't matter that much because she was thinking of going to this tennis ranch in Scottsdale with John Newcombe. "Jealous?"

He walked back to his own apartment, sometimes as late as midnight in the middle of the week. One night he remembered to look for his chain in the uncut grass under the flowering cherry. But as he squatted to unfasten the lock he couldn't remember the combination. He had one of those blank moments when he knew if he waited for it, the name, or in this case a set of numbers, would come back. Presto. But his thighs ached and he abandoned it.

Every time he visited her after that he tried to remember his combination in the grass. Trying to remember was a game and he refused to look up the card he had with the numbers written down. It annoyed him he couldn't recall three numbers memorized six months earlier. His business was to remember numbers the way a squash player remembers angles. "Hey, Ben, can we live with these numbers?" Figures in his world were numbers — just as chairmen were chairpersons. (The salespeople at meetings who were women insisted on the title.) At lunch he would sometimes grow absent, not hear his gesturing companion, and listen instead like a safe-cracker for the tiny sounds of tumbling digits. Once over Sanka he thought he smelled freshly cut grass, and dog urine. He sniffed his cup. By May the cherry blossoms had all gone.

On a Sunday morning that month he phoned to ask if she

wanted to try for a court. "I've got on an apron and pancakes," she said. "Thought you were coming over." He'd forgotten. "If you'd rather play tennis," she told him, "go ahead." He thought it sounded like a test, so he apologized and walked over in his Adidas and whites and had pancakes. He enjoyed them more than he expected to, and spilled syrup on his shorts.

When she was running hot water over the stain he removed the rest of his clothes and waited for her in bed. Listening to her toothbrush he got up and drew the curtains closed on their cedar rings. As soon as she came into the room smelling of Dial and Ultrabrite he gathered her long, thick hair in his hand and bit the back of her neck. "That's how the Japanese do it," he growled. "Bullshit," she said. "They do it like this." He laughed. They both made big bellies and denounced pancakes as disgusting and probably immoral. "Think of the squatters starving in Calcutta," he told her. She sighed. "Mother Teresa isn't getting *me*," she said. "Besides, she only takes movie stars and pop singers." Standing there on a little rug from Jakarta they rubbed their stomachs together like inflated beach balls. He looked down her back and admired the long dark leg, bent at the knee, poised on its toes. "You exotic cunts are all alike," he said. "You'll go down on your back for a pancake."

Afterwards, lying there, they drifted off. The Dutch clock in the kitchen went cuckoo eleven times. Helpless with laughter she turned to him with love in her eyes. "I ought to tell you," she said.

She said the only time she'd ever gone out with a guy she didn't know was last night on a stupid date her friend Katie at work had set up. She gave this guy her number, and when he phoned he asked did she remember him from August? "I didn't remember him at all. It was a really stupid date." He picked her up in his brother's Rambler, she said, with these spotty seatcovers that felt Mexican to sit on. All he could talk about was when he was going to get a Mazda and how great she looked, but he kept saying it in the stupidest way, like she was a Liberty scarf or a packet of spangled panty hose. Besides, he didn't even know her. They went to Humphrey's, which was stupid because he said he couldn't afford the appetizers. She didn't care if she had an appetizer or not, but why go to a restaurant you can't afford in the first place? The view maybe. Or maybe he was razzing her. "I ended up ordering stuffed sole and I *hate* fish. He kept asking me the stupidest questions." Like what was her favourite food? Or were the colour of the sheets on her bed mauve like her blouse? And how come she wore her hair behind her ears, or did it just go that way? "This guy is supposedly a university graduate in Forestry. He turned me right off." They ended up at a Whitecaps' game under the Dome and sat in seats a mile up in Section 32, which was stupid because you couldn't see the game and he wouldn't move to better seats that were empty.

"God, he was a joke! His conversation consisted of what he was having, like, for lunch at the plywood plant where he's supposedly learning management." She snorted with laughter at the recollection, and the bed shook gently. "Fruitcake! It was insane. The only interesting thing he said all night was he knew Doug's sister, or Doug's cousin, or Doug's *something* — of Doug and the Slugs. And she wants to start a band called Movement. On the way home I could hardly listen to him. He asked me did I want to go someplace for coffee and dessert? No. Could he kiss me goodnight? No. Could he maybe see me again because, well, he was really intrigued by somebody different? No. It was stupid, really stupid."

She took his hand and placed it fondly on her stomach. "This morning I decided that's the last time I go out with anybody who isn't a friend of mine already."

Then she said, "A trust company's funny for friends like Katie. I mean I really like Katie, but our tastes are just different. She's younger I guess." She thought awhile. "I'm tired of withdrawals and standing up all day." She lay back and stared at the old schooner reproduced a hundred times in the wall-paper. "The men get careers. The girls just disappear. At a trust company you either quit or get shoved off to another branch. I'd like to get into mortgages."

He listened to what she told him. "I'm glad you're seeing other men," he said. "But this guy sounds like a liability."

She laughed. "Isn't that what you wanted?"

"What."

"I feel guilty, though. That's why I lied about breakfast. I wanted to make it up to you."

He said, "I thought my memory was going." And told her about forgetting his combination around her tree outside.

She found this touching, the lock with no Norco to mind, and they slept until the cuckoo roused them at noon. They woke up smiling. He looked into her dark eyes. "You exotic cunts," he said. He made her breast large by lifting it like a custard. "Is this," she asked, "what losing your memory does for an appetite?" Later, on their way out to a court in the park, she bent down in her white tennis dress and played in the grass with his numbers. She was twenty-three.

He remembered her birthday in June when she turned twenty-four. He bought her roses, dinner and a modest remembrance. "I've never *kept* a diary," she said. "Keep it in your vault," he warned her. In July when he turned thirty-two she hired a chauffeured limousine and stopped by his office tower to pick him up. Last year she hadn't done anything she said on account of her being in Europe. "Besides, I didn't know you as well."

He told her it was pricey on her salary to be treating him to this. She took him to the Four Seasons for Broiled Sockeye under Bernaise Sauce (she had Veal Oscar) and afterwards told the chauffeur to drive them up the mountain. They parked at an angle on Hollyburn and looked down at the lit-up freighters and city. She handed the driver, who even wore a chauffeur's cap, a bunch of dinner mints. They all gazed down and listened to old Rock 'n' Roll songs on speakers hidden inside the grey-flannel roof. She had requested this particular tape because she thought he'd remember the songs. "Hey," he laughed. "I'm not your father." He sank back into the upholstery smoking her Schimmelpenninck cigars. "This evening must have cost you a month's salary," he said. "About," she shrugged. "Anyway, I'm not going anywhere this year. I told John Newcombe to buzz off." There was a chance she might get out of telling soon, into a desk job. She looked down over the sparkling world, up into the firmament. A group called The Platters were singing *My need is such, I pretend too much, I'm lonely but no one can tell. . . .* "I really like these old songs," she said. On their way back down to the bridge she asked the chauffeur to park at Ambleside, where they walked barefoot in the black sand. The Beatles crooned through the rolled-down windows of Yesterday, and the driver's cigar glowed like a paper lantern.

In August she took local tennis lessons to get rid of the loop in her serve and to improve her footwork. After dinner they often met in the park to play a set before dusk. She was a gifted athlete and beat him more often than he liked. Later on they walked to Ping Pong's on Altamira and had Italian ice cream in small aluminum dishes. She said that after tennis with him, and the hour and a half lesson before that, she could eat a whole tureen of Malaga. But she kept a paring knife handy to remind her of the destiny of fat girls. Meryl Streep had a peach and cabbage diet she admired.

In October he dropped into Canada Trust to buy American Express travellers cheques, waved at her behind a till, and went away on his holidays to Hawaii. Not, however, before catching sight of a thin boy up the street with a ten-speed Norco. "This is mine," he said, grabbing the saddle. The thin boy and his friends turned to him with avid curiosity. He had jay-walked through four lanes of rush-hour traffic to nab the thief, who had his knee hooked over the crossbar.

The next day he flew to Honolulu in need of rest and recuperation. The Norco was not his at all. The pedals had toe-straps and the saddle under his hand felt bony it was so narrow. He apologized to the boy who just smirked. His friends, sea cadets, laughed abusively. That evening, packing his suitcase, he phoned her and let the phone whir nine, ten times before hanging up. He wondered if he had the right number, for the exchange he reached sounded custodial and distant.

It was a pleasure to think it was raining at home. He sunbathed on Waikiki, toured a few clubs, bought himself white loafers, and then flew to Maui for the last week of his holidays. In Lahina, where he stayed at the Pioneer Inn, he struck it lucky with the piano player downstairs, a green-eyed doctor on leave from Los Angeles playing her way through the islands. She was living on a thirty-foot Yamaha with her poet husband. Meeting her was lucky because of the girl she introduced him to, her husband's flaxen-haired sister, who served beer in the same pub. Together they all went sailing one day to Molakai, the old leper island across the strait. They were into the sauce. The blonde poet sucked unlit Lucky Strikes and pointed out where the whale pods arrived in January, asking Ben if he knew *Typee*. He hadn't heard of it. Just off a coral reef on Molakai they dropped their sails and the rest of their clothing. He and the poet cooked frankfurters over propane in the galley, rubbed Coppertone into the girls' backs, and gave them the whole day off. The doctor asked herself why she was playing the piano in a bar every night when they still had savings. She laughed. Her sister-in-law, tanned dark from spending every afternoon in the sun, and before this two years in Africa, said, "I hope we can hang around these islands forever." She'd just finished teaching with the Peace Corps in Nigeria, where her eyes had been opened. He gazed a little drunkenly into her blue irises. She sliced pieces of watermelon and he admired her pale gardenia breasts. "Over there," she concluded, "we're definitely in a minority." The three strangers mentioned books they were reading, and he felt left out. The doctor's breasts perked up like baby owls. The poet put his head in her lap and bit into the flesh of his watermelon rind. He gave Ben a volume of his verse to look through, neatly cut stanzas of long lines and no punctuation, each poem addressed to a different girl whose name always began with I. Iris, Ivy, Ianthe,

Isadora, Irene. . . ''All Greek,'' said the poet. ''All tried and true.'' He put aside his rind and spoke earnestly to his new friend. ''Every woman has a year in her life,'' he said, ''month, week, even — dare I whisper it — a day, when she reaches a summit of perfection, a rare point in time like a peak in the Sierras, when she's neither child nor adult in any strict sense, and from which her body will begin to slide imperceptibly away. This is a sexist observation, Benjamin, certainly not a balanced one, because in toto a woman is a whole mountain range.'' He smiled appreciatively at his dozing wife. And later on, dopey with sun, he turned to his sister and murmured, ''What you noticed in Africa, Hel, was there're lots more dark women in the world than light.'' To go swimming — in water as inviting as Helen's eyes — they hung an aluminum ladder off the stern and snorkelled down to coral.

Returning to Vancouver he learned she was planning to move at the end of November. Because of the recession more vacancies existed now than when she'd taken her present apartment. The new place, she told him, had a small view of the bay and she was surprised to be taking a step *up* in the world since her real reason for moving was the cheaper rent. She was also checking out a sales job at a downtown radio station. They were looking, she'd heard, for better balance in their staff, and she guessed a woman who was ethnic might have a fair chance of success. She rented a U-Haul and he helped her park it. Her heaviest things were a sofa and the bricks she used to make a board planter. He took apart her bed and found the futon lighter to tote than the kitchen clock.

In one of the last boxes to be loaded into the elevator, lying among herb jars and a rolling pin, was the diary he'd given her. Riding down alone he opened it to see if she ever used it. Most pages that year were blank. There were a few entries like *Went swimming today at Aquatic Center with Katie, promised myself exercise classes.* And *Met Ben downtown to see Stardust Memories, with supper afterwards at Las Tapas. Home for a juicy something, but it wasn't a screw, both bushed. He went home.* The longest entry read *Sometimes I feel like a mistake. Loneliness is a bad city inside you. I don't understand how so much can be going on with so many people doing it and I have nothing to do with anything except gloom. Bought a blouse at the Bay.*

That night to ease the transition she stayed over at his place. She'd forgotten how big his apartment was and what a view of the park he had, even in the rain. She loved his plants, his white rattan furniture, his full refrigerator. She remembered the Markgraf prints and the decanter of sherry. They drank some sherry. "Everything's so magic here," she said. "I envy your touch." He smiled like a pirate, his dark hair shorter than Richard Gere's by a businessman's inch. Later she woke up beside him in bed and asked what he was reading. "Melville," he said. "The Greenpeace Grandaddy who wrote *Moby Dick.*" Outside on the balcony the cold rain was puddling, but inside by the bleached glow of his chrome lamp it was warm.

"I love the south seas," she said, snuggling closer to the light.

At a meeting that year before Christmas he tried to remember the phone number of her old apartment. He wrote down different combinations of the last four digits, and none looked right. He remembered the prefix all right since it was the same as his own. That evening he phoned her new number and she seemed surprised to hear from him. He told her he'd been away on trips to Toronto and Montreal trying to make his boss some money. Tomorrow he was going to Calgary to see if he could make some more. And her? "Okay, I guess. Still at the Trust Company." An aunt of hers from Rotterdam was coming for Christmas, and tonight she was picking her up at the airport, in a new old car she'd bought from a friend at work. "Do you know anything about Crickets?" she asked. "Don't tell me if you do." She wondered when they would see each other again. "Over New Year's," he promised. "When I get my act together." She told him she had recently had her legs waxed. "Let me tell you," she said.

He ran into her in March at the tennis courts. He was driving home and saw her playing, striding into the ball with litheness and grace. Her brown limbs shone under her white tennis dress, and her brief blue anklets flew over the green sunny asphalt. She saw him at the fence and waved. Azalea and magnolia blossoms filled the air. When it was her turn to serve she corralled the lime Dunlops at her feet and spoke through the wire. ''Katie,'' she said, ''is now better than I am. She took lessons in Colorado.'' He told her she looked pretty good herself. She smiled shyly. ''This year I'm definitely going to Arizona, in October.'' Hooking her finger in the mesh she asked him how he was. He said he figured the recession had finallly bottomed out and things were on their way back up.

''You forget my number or what?'' she said.

He didn't pretend he had forgotten it, and rattled it off. She laughed. ''That's my old number,'' she said.

''Is it?'' He seemed pleased.

She looked relieved. He took down her new number again and said he would call.

A week later driving by her old building he stopped along the No Parking curb and switched on his emergency flasher. The Japanese cherry was in full flower. He had thought of it again at a performance of *Madama Butterfly* the other night with a lawyer he'd met in January at a party. He got out of his car and crossed over to the grass. He knelt down in the fallen blossoms and picked up his lock and chain. But the face was encrusted with rust so thick he couldn't dial the numbers in either direction, not even a hair.

Born in New Jersey in 1931, JANE RULE came to the Canadian Westcoast aged 25. After two or three domiciles in the Point Grey area of the city (when she was associated with the University of British Columbia) she moved to the Gulf Island of Galiano. She thus remains, nearly thirty years later, still within the metropolitan vortex of the city of Vancouver. The author of seven volumes of fiction and the critical work, *Lesbian Images*, her latest books are a collection of essays, *A Hot-Eyed Moderate* and a fiction work, *Inland Passage and Other Stories.*

JANE RULE

Blessed Are The Dead

"Such a satisfying death!" Martin said, shaking out the *Vancouver Sun* and settling more comfortably in his chair. "Even in the eulogies, all his sins are being remembered."

"Are we going to the funeral?" Lily asked, handing him a very much thinned scotch.

"I wouldn't miss it, would you? There will be all the children and mistresses of the first marriage, the second Mrs. Kurr with all her children and all the — what does one call them? — companions of the second 'open marriage', various bartenders and lawyers: a bloody circus!"

"You haven't spoken to him for five years," Lily said.

"The very best reason not to miss the opportunity to cut him dead one last time."

"Doesn't it scare you to be that callous?"

"Lily, my skin is as thin as my old mother's. I quiver with feeling. How often in a life do we experience for ourselves a sense that — what's that wonderful line in Christopher Fry? — that the brick has been 'richly deserved and divinely delivered." Most drunken, whoring old buggers are rewarded with appointments to the bench and life into the nineties. I feel on the edge of conversion."

"As a died-again Christian?" Lily asked.

"That's going too far, of course. It's more a Sunday school nostalgia," Martin admitted, "when I really did believe bastards like Wally Kurr would be struck dead. I've lived so many years with irony, with knowing it's more likely that boy scouts like me would drop dead at fifty, snow shovel in hand, after a life of one watered down scotch before dinner, a workout three times a week, and a cigar on my birthday. Now, even if I die on Friday of smug pleasure at his funeral, I'll still have the satisfaction of having outlived him."

"He's the first one, isn't he?" Lily mused, "if you don't count Clara Kurr's suicide or Jim Wilson's plane crash."

"The first what?"

"One of us to . . . just die."

"Well, there're your parents and my father. . . "

"I mean, our age, more or less. Wally was a year ahead of me at UBC."

"And two years behind me. He was only forty-eight," Martin said, checking the paper. "You know, I think we ought to go out for dinner and celebrate the fact that there's some justice left in the world."

"The way to get a man to go out to dinner is to put him on a diet. Then he's willing to make anything a cause for celebration: an old friend's death, a daughter's abortion."

"Wally Kurr was never really a friend of mine, and we don't have a daughter and I didn't know I was on a diet."

"Daughter-in-law."

"It's not the same thing," Martin said. "I'm perfectly willing to celebrate not having a daughter. Imagine living in incestuous terror for nearly twenty years of your life!"

"Oh, Martin."

"Now, none of that fashionable feminist revulsion. Husbands don't like it at all."

"I'll go out to dinner as long as it's not the Club," Lily said.

"But don't you like to see your friends?"

"They're your friends."

"Friends are friends, Lily, and they are the best insurance there is for you against finding the company of your husband a bore."

"You've never bored me," Lily said.

"Where would you like to go?"

"The Club," she answered. "I'll have to change."

Martin preferred to be recognized in public, and he could count on that only at the Faculty Club. Elsewhere Lily attracted admiring attention because of her Sunday talk show on Channel 2. Neither of them would be much noticed a hundred miles or more from Vancouver unless they went where Vancouverites go or to an academic symposium. Martin had an international reputation among a limited number of scholars for his work on the nature of tragi-comedy, its important Christian underpinnings.

"It's still perfectly acceptable to write about Christianity as long as you aren't one" was Martin's social explanation, particularly at Lily's studio parties which were short on professors and long on people who did things (as opposed to teaching them or writing about them).

Lily did allow a certain number of writers on her talk show, mostly in deference to Martin's taste. As a breed, they didn't interview well, either monosyllabic or uninterruptable, vain about everything but their looks, probably because they spent most of their time with their backs to the world.

"I really think people who care about posterity should wait for it," she said.

As a lecturer as well as a scholar, Martin felt he had the best of both worlds, the here and the hereafter, of which he had a clear picture in his mind. It was a library in which his book, *The Nature of Grace, a Study of Tragi-Comedy*, was prominently displayed. It was such a concrete reassurance against the unimaginable faces of his great-great-grandchildren about whom he knew only the one thing: they would remember him.

Martin finished his scotch and stood to greet his expensively dressed wife who wore, on a silk suit her public had not yet seen, the Tony Cavelti pin he had given her on their last anniversary.

"Why on earth did we ever have children?" he asked her.

"How else would you know how to enjoy being free of them?" she asked him.

"If either of my sons had ruined your figure, I would have murdered them in their cribs. As it is, I don't harbor an ounce of ill will toward them."

Martin held the door of the Mercedes Lily had given him for an anniversary present several years ago and felt the satisfaction of knowing that he could sell it now for more than she had paid for it. With the house mortgage paid off, holidays already scheduled (Mexico for Christmas, England in May), Martin and Lily were on the good side of these bad times.

As they drove along the shore, the late sun shone on picnicking families at the beach, on freighters at anchor waiting for berths in the inner harbour; on sailboats, on the water itself, golden and slate grey. The bushes were still in wonderfully vulgar bloom in the rose garden, but the flag by the Faculty Club was at half mast.

"Not for Wally!" Martin exclaimed.

"He was a graduate," Lily reminded him.

"We don't lower the flag for every graduate! We'd have to leave it there permanently. Maybe someone's shot the Prime Minister."

"We aren't in Texas," Lily said.

A notice at the front desk informed them that the lowered flag was, indeed, for Wallace Kurr.

"You weren't all that glum at the space he took up on the front page," Lily reminded him, "and, after all, we're eating out in his honour."

"But the flag is for prominent, not notorious citizens."

"They're more or less indistinguishable."

Here their conversation was interrupted by greetings from Martin's colleagues and their wives, rather more of them than Martin had expected on a week night until he remembered that there was a cocktail party sheduled in the lower lounge for a retiring dean whom Martin despised.

"Oh God, now that we're here, I suppose we should just . . . nod in."

But, of course, there was no nodding in on such occasions. The speeches had just begun.

Whyever had he let Lily give in to him about coming here where such pomposities as this could so often override conviviality? Looking at the numbers in the room, Martin worried that he would not get a table, certainly not a good table, in the dining room. Nearly everyone here was old enough not to be leashed to a babysitter and could easily stay on. Perhaps the thing to do was to persuade Chester and Margerie over there to go downtown with them for dinner.

Oh, these deadly phrases, "inspiring mentor", "distinguished contribution", for a man who had been elevated to dean in order to spare him and his department the embarrassment of dwindling enrollment in his ill prepared and haltingly presented lectures, to get rid of his reactionary presence on committees. It was as ridiculous as lowering the flag for Wally.

Yet Martin's basic satisfaction reasserted itself at the thought of Wally, at this very moment a cold corpse waiting for flames or worms. Retirement after all was a little death, this ceremony a dress rehearsal, at which the corpse, unlike the bride, was present.

It was too much to hope that the parting gift would be something witty and original like, say, a goldfish bowl or a spittoon. Occasionally a man with a confessed hobby got a fishing rod or some golf clubs, but this fellow was handed his retirement on the expected silver platter, unsuitable for either carving turkey or handing round martinis, its only function to be cleaned.

Because they were at the back of the room, Martin and Lily did get a table, a window table, in the dining room, and Chester and Margerie, whom they'd known since their undergraduate days, came to join them.

"What a surprise!" Chester said. "I thought such politicking was beneath you."

"An honest mistake," Martin explained. "We came over to celebrate the just demise of Wally Kurr."

"Ah, Wally," Margerie said. "He was my first rabbit test."

"I guess, when you live in the fast lane, you get there more quickly," Chester observed mildly.

"He was not in the fast lane," Martin said. "He's been

right off the rails for years."

"You've never forgiven him Clara's suicide, have you?" Margerie asked.

"If I had to list the number of things that I haven't forgiven Wally, that nobody should forgive Wally, we'd be here all night. Shall we start with snails?"

"Lovely," Lily agreed.

"It says here 'escargot'."

"Have we been speaking French?" Martin asked.

"Martin is only purely bilingual," Lily reminded them.

"Otherwise we'll get the English equivalent to *joual*."

"Snails it is," Chester agreed. "I'm sure that's what Peter Trudeau eats in Toronto."

"When we saw the flag, Martin wondered if he'd been shot."

"Who decides about that flag, Chester?" Martin demanded.

"A committee," Chester answered from behind the wine list.

"Everybody knew Wally," Margerie said. "After all."

"Without Wally the local papers would have had to shut down for lack of news," Chester said.

"For lack of scandal."

"The difference?" Lily asked. "Martin's faith in destiny has been restored tonight."

"Surely not?" Chester looked at Martin.

"No, but still it is wonderful to see justice with her sweet, impartial face visit this planet. She is not after all in permanent eclipse."

"Death's boatman takes no bribe, nor brings E'vn skilled Prometheus back from Hades' shore," Chester intoned in his unfortunate tenor.

"Is it really necessary to gloat?" Margerie asked. "What about his present wife and all those children? Where's the justice for them?"

"He settled all his property on her before the last time he declared bankruptcy, and that's over two years ago, plenty of time for him to have dealt himself back into the game."

"Were you a tiny bit jealous of him, Martin?"

"If I was, I am no longer. May he rest in peace," Martin said, raising his glass.

"Were you really ever jealous of Wally?" Lily asked on their way home.

"Why is it that women have always excused Wally?" he asked in return. "I suppose it's understandable that a nice girl like Margerie would go to bed with him when she was nineteen. She didn't know any better. But why defend him now?"

"He died good looking and, you think, rich."

"Good looking? He was as thin as a stork."

Lily was tactfully silent.

The phone was ringing as they walked in the door. Lily answered it, listened for a moment, raised her eyebrows, and then said, "Just a minute. He's right here." She put her hand over the receiver and said, "It's Joan Kurr."

"I don't even know her," Martin mouthed frantically.

Lily shrugged and held the phone out to him.

"Yes?" he said, he hoped with some sympathy in his tone.

Then, after a long pause, he said, "Yes," again, and it came out more like a reluctant admission of guilt.

When he hung up the phone, Martin said in disbelief, "Do you know what I've just agreed to do? I've just agreed to be one of the pall bearers!"

"You were an usher in his first wedding," Lily reminded him.

"For Clara's sake," he protested.

"And now for Joan's?"

"It isn't her idea. It was Wally's, one of his mortal broodings after Clara died, no doubt."

"Well, you did want to go to the funeral anyway."

"But not as his . . . accomplice!"

"He's dead, after all."

"O death, where is thy sting. O grave where is thy victory?"

"Oh, Martin, where is your sense of humour?"

Martin flung himself into a chair, stared at the empty fireplace and said, "How could he do this to me?" silently adding *again*.

Martin, dressed in his only three piece suit, which was dark grey, expected to be the only respectable man at the coffin. He did not worry about the safety of his wallet or his watch, for Wally's friends would be in the upper echelon of crooks and gamblers who managed real estate in the city, sporting gold nuggets from their own mines on their watch chains. He did worry about his own good name among them in the report of this religious farce in the evening paper.

Having looked up the burial service in the prayer book, Martin discovered that the church, probably in times when the dead were buried in the church yard, was suggested only in inclement weather for a ritual intended for the graveside. It was a cloudy day.

What choices among the ironies would the minister fall upon? "He heapeth up riches, and cannot tell who shall gather them" or "Raise us from the death of sin unto the life of righteousness" or — and he read this one out to Lily as she was putting on her hat — "make me not a rebuke unto the foolish."

"Which would be intended for us, no doubt," Lily observed.

Even though they arrived early, finding a parking place was difficult. Martin cursed the limousines which dwarfed his beloved Mercedes, but he was able to squeeze into a place that a Lincoln had just failed to negotiate. His moral superiority was intact.

"Do try not to look smug," Lily said. "I'll save you a seat on the aisle."

Martin turned to see that the other men loitering on the steps waiting for direction as pall bearers were all known to him not from the gossip columns but from the university, a classmate who had become a doctor, the president of Wally's own class, a quite respectable corporation lawyer, the owner of a fish-packing company who had also been an usher at Wally's first wedding.

He said to Martin, "To tell the truth, I wouldn't be here if Mrs. Kurr hadn't specifically asked me. . . "

One by one each confessed to a similar uncertainty, not having seen Wally in years, but each also felt an uneasy loyalty to those old ties of friendship when they had been young together, poaching on each other's female territory, wrecking each other's cars, predicting ill-favoured futures for each other, and standing up at each other's weddings.

Nobody wanted to say what they all probably assumed, that Wally had no other friends. Martin tried to remember if he'd felt any less cynical and out of place at Wally's wedding. Martin had agreed to that only because he'd been in love with Clara himself and didn't want anyone else to know it. But what humiliation had he to cover up here that made him agree to be in this bewildered company?

Between the funeral director and the minister, they were soon instructed on their simple duties and could join the crowd moving into the church.

"Who are all these people?" Martin muttered to Lily, for the church was full.

As he himself had facetiously predicted, they were all Wally's old loves and his children. Also there were both prominent crooks and their bankers with their second and third wives. Across the church Martin spotted Chester and Margerie who would witness his embarrassment with some amusement.

Then he eyed the coffin, resting below the altar banked with pretentious flowers, which he and the comrades of his youth were to bear away.

"Behold, I shew you a mystery; we shall not all sleep, but we shall be changed in a moment, in a twinkling of an eye, at the last trump; for the trumpet shall sound, and the dead shall be raised incorruptible. . . "

Martin snorted loudly. What they should have planned to do was drop the coffin in the aisle and let the body roll out for all to see the essentially corrupted remains of Wally Kurr, the womanizer, the crook, the killer, for he had killed Clara as surely as if he'd shot her himself.

Yet Martin found himself chanting, along with hundreds of other unbelievers, "Christ, have mercy on us." And, sharing a hymnal with Lily, he raised his voice to sing, "Rock of Ages, cleft for me. . . " and pondered the lines, "All for sin could not atone/Thou must save and thou alone. . . "

Where was the justice in all this? Though Martin believed no more in hell than in heaven, if he had to be burdened with Christian imagery, surely there should be a little more crackling of flames for this particular sinner.

At the end of the final prayer, Martin rose with the other men and walked up the aisle to the coffin. Unrehearsed and unaccustomed to manual tasks, they were clumsy with the flowers, clumsier still lifting the coffin and getting it down the steps, though it wasn't really very heavy. By this time Martin was too anxious not to make a fool of himself to think of making a fool of Wally Kurr's corpse. When the men had the coffin on the straightaway of the aisle, they figured out the necessity of walking in step, and Martin had a sudden sense of the theatrical dignity of their task. So strong was the form that, though he believed not at all in redemption, he knew he and the others had become agents of grace, only needing to bear and forbear to the grave to defeat completely the justice he had come to witness.

As mechanical, as arbitrary as any device in the tragi-comedies he had studied so long, Martin, the righteous man, shouldered his part of the burden of body and box out to the waiting hearse, then out of the hearse over the uncertain turf of the cemetery to the grave site on which a gentle rain began appropriately to fall.

Among the weeping women, including Margerie and Lily, Martin stood without solace.

"From henceforth blessed are the dead. . . "

DAVID WATMOUGH arrived in New York as a Cornish emigrant in 1952 and found himself a resident of Vancouver ten years later. Since then the fifty-nine year-old author has produced six volumes of fiction with a seventh slated for publication during Expo year. His most recent works have been the fiction volumes *The Connecticut Countess,* and *Fury*, and an account of opera growth in Western Canada, *The Unlikely Pioneer*. He has made his home in the Kitsilano district of the city for the past 24 years.

DAVID WATMOUGH

Vancouver Summer Pudding

Take a bowl of fresh ripe blackberries adding sugar to taste. Around the interior of bowl lay slices of thinly cut white sandwich bread. Lay further slices across open top of bowl thus covering the fruit. Cover with greaseproof paper and a plate small enough to fit inside of bowl rim and on top of greaseproof. Then put either old-fashioned flat-iron or two or three bricks as weights on plate. Place bowl in refrigerator for thirty-six hours. Take bowl out, remove weights, and turn upside down on serving platter. The result should be a bowl-shaped pudding with exterior bread slices now molded into pudding shape and saturated with fruit juices from the blackberries. Serve in cut portions and add whipped cream.

We first noticed Richard and Anna when blackberry picking in Vancouver's Jericho Park on a hot day at the tail end of July. Ken and I were equipped simply with plastic bags from the nearby Safeway. They were prone to puncture on the bramble thorns so that we had to be extra careful in holding them high above the leaves when craning for the tall-growing fruit or away from the runners which disappeared into the long grass where we knew that there were yet more berries in plentiful supply.

But the Cobhams were altogether more professional. For one thing they carried walking sticks which they used with their handles inverted to lower some of the higher growing berries. And they put their blackberries into stiff straw baskets, the likes of which I hadn't seen since leaving England thirty years earlier. Even their apparel accorded better with berry collecting than did our garments. Then we were trying to combine this operation with walking two dogs, and Ken had come straight from the university campus and was wearing his teaching clothes. I was imprudently wearing an easily stained white shirt with short sleeves which left my arms readily vulnerable to savage scratching from the briars all about us.

The four of us were not alone. The edges of the park near the pond sites were adjacent to an old people's home and there were several of its inmates busily picking for the tarts and pies which would remind some of them of distant childhoods and prairie summers — for many, I had learned on our regular dogwalks, were retired Saskatchewan and Alberta farmers; immigrants, like me, to British Columbia. The bond was the past — and the special pleasure of harvesting things that mankind had not cultivated. There was a bent old man in a black beret with a white-haired wife with gnarled, clawing hands, joined in the mute intensity of their husbandry. And at one small, isolated patch, a frail, grand-motherly person frantically picking for a lazier generation (or so I imagined) who would visit on Sundays, eagerly wolf a piece of homemade pie but talk of jogging and gymns.

But it wasn't the oldsters who had ultimately engaged our attention; nor the unruly kids who bent and broke a hundred tangled vines to pick a random berry and pop it between stained lips before passing, like a herd of giraffes, to the next unravaged clump. No, our interest was fired by this youngish couple who were working just a little apart from each other, but shouting every now and then to indicate fresh blackberries along the narrow path.

It was from her calling to him that I realised she was not a native English-speaker. But it was not, in fact, until a second encounter at a different site the following week that I learned she was German and that she was Anna, and he Richard and that their married name was Cobham. It was Ken who collected all that information — while I was busy rounding up an errant Springer spaniel puppy from the railway tracks under the Burrard bridge and holding on to a straining Norwegian Elkhound who rarely agreed with me over directions to take.

If it had been hot when picking at Jericho it seemed doubly so at this spot which was slightly further from any breeze from the sea. Here the brambles grew like breakers of greenery amid a sea of masonry and concrete which in turn threw the heat waves back at those who walked along the cinder path. I told a sweating Ken that I could scarcely remember when a cloud last scudded eastward across that remorseless sky. The vast sprawl of Vancouver wilted under the exigent heat as it grew progressively dusty and untidy. The hot days of sun brought crowds to the parched lawns of the city parks for which a niggardly council had refused sprinklers. The containers of waste were never sufficiently emptied to the point were the litter at their base was completely removed. Irresponsible dogowners allowed their animals to roam freely and deposit excrement where tanned youths and little children played. Drains smelled and the still air of the beaches was laced with unpleasant odors from the exposed giant sewers that reached out to sea. Not so privately, I declared our usually attractive city a mess and I can testify that every blackberry picked during those oppressive afternoons was washed, and washed, and washed again.

When a perspiring and irate me caught up with Ken after chasing Leila and lugging Leif up the steep railroad embankment I came across the three of them, picking and animatedly chatting. The bushes where they stood were particularly dusty and there was an unpleasant abundance of yellowing sheets of discarded newspapers impaled on various bushes and shrubs. It was not an attractive spot but the blackberries grew on both sides of the trail and were large and ripe and plentiful. Nobody else seemed to have discovered the place for a quick glance assured me there were none of those diminutive empty cups, paler than the surrounding greenery, as telltale evidence of berries picked from the same bushes.

I gave the Cobhams much closer scrutiny than the bushes as Ken introduced us and conversation picked up once more. The woman, Anna, now that I knew she was German, took on distinctly Nordic characteristics. She was blonde-haired, blue-eyed, and in her blue check blouse and denim skirt, looked cool and smart in spite of the heat and her exertion. I noticed when she picked berries above her that her armpits were unshaven — although her brown legs disappearing stockingless into loafers, were smooth enough. She was an ex-kindergarten teacher, I learned, and her husband a geneticist at the University of British Columbia. He had been born in Bristol and still had a vestigial British accent although his family, apparently, had moved to BC when he was a highschool student. I estimated they were both in their early thirties. They lived only six blocks from us in Kitsilano.

An adonis Richard Cobham was not. But what I did find appealing was his indubitable charm. The ready grin under the shock of unruly hair which fell across his forehead, shared pride of place with sparkling eyes. He also owned to a snub nose and a slim body. The latter, I sensed, spelled a questing energy which appeared consonant with his frequent spurts of laughter. Later I was to construe all that winsome youthfulness in quite another way, but not as we stood there, the four of us, playfully competing for the number of blackberries we were able to gather. Richard had the fullest basket — then he had the tallest reach and was the fastest at picking the fruit from its thorny branches. And all the time he talked, including me now in his audience.

"Anna is a lousy cook, in spite of her being European. I think that's why she went to Montreal where I met her. By *their* standards and their ghastly pig pie — that *tourtière* — she's haute cuisine, cordon blue, anything you bloody well like! Have either of you ever had that horrible disappointment in Quebec? You look at a menu and there it all is, just as you'd find *à la carte* in Beaune or Bordeaux. Until the stuff arrives on the table and you find the French language has been camouflaging crappy old Canadian "greasey spoon". What a fucking disappointment when that first happens to you!" "Richard! Please mind your language. Not everyone appreciates your cussing."

We both reassured her that it didn't matter. It was obvious that it didn't matter to Richard either. Certainly she wasn't going to deter him or his vocabulary.

"Anyway, compared to *une tarte de bleuets Gaspésienne* her blackberry flan is better than a slab of shit. You guys must come over and try it. She won't mind trying her feeble culinary skills before a couple of men, will you my love?" Anna grinned ruefully. "You don't cook?" she asked me. "Only water," I told her. "Ken does it all. Mind you," I added quickly, "we both make a point of not choosing friends for their cooking talents. Nor for their athletic prowess, arable skills, fecundity or nautical abilities, come to that."

They both laughed and I was relieved. I didn't like seeing a man putting down his wife — or vice versa. But I also noticed that my words inspired Mr. Richard Cobham to give us an extra sizing up. I wondered just how much Ken had told them about us before I had arrived with the dogs. I was pretty sure it was very little, knowing Ken. . . .

"And cards, too, I hope," Richard supplemented, as his questing look embraced my roommate as well as myself. "Anna and I are hopeless at all card games — and that includes scrabble, monopoly and bloody bridge."

"We shoot people and bury them under the kitchen floor if they arrive at our house even *carrying* a deck of cards," I told him.

Richard may not have liked cards but it was very evident that he loved playing games — English parlor games.

"OK" he shouted (then he rarely spoke more quietly out there in the open air) "Let's see what else we can agree on. How about Anna's stepmother — the biggest bitch in Christendom. You must've read about her. She's in the Guiness Book for bitchery!"

"Darling, don't be so extravagant," Anna pleaded. "You'll have both Ken and Davey thinking you're madder than you really are."

"I really am amazed that no one has found this lot of blackberries before us,'' Ken said pacifically.

''People are blind,'' Richard said roughly. ''And bloody stupid to boot. They don't only miss blackberries, though. They let the goddamn Americans go on preparing to blow up the world.'' He sounded so savage, in fact, that I stopped picking — and as I did so, let a particularly thorny bramble swing back and slash my bare arm which was upraised to protect my face. Although we stood in the shade the air was still warm and motionless: nevertheless I felt the extra warmth immediately upon my exposed skin. I looked down. A rash of red beads burgeoned as the scratch flowered into bloody blossom.

Richard was at once all anxiety. ''Jesus! That looks nasty! Here, use this.'' He pulled a Kleenex pack from the army satchel at his feet. But his wife was at his side in an instant. She, too, rummaged in the bag and brought out a small bottle of Dettol, surgical cotton and a package of Elastoplasts.

She pushed her husband aside. ''Here, let me have a look.''

''It doesn't hurt,'' I told her as she wiped away the first installment of blood and then applied the disinfectant.

''And I'm sure it's clean,'' I added.

''You can't be too careful,'' she warned. ''Anyway, I took first-aid once and I love to practice. Ask Richard. The smallest cut and I've got him swathed in bandages.''

''Thank God I'm a hypochondriac,'' he said with another grin.

''It has kept our marriage together for six years. She's a frustrated doctor, you see — and I'm a potentially perpetual patient. It works beautifully.''

She put the largest Elastoplast over the surgical wool so that my scratch was entirely covered. ''That's how *he* puts it,'' she said, looking up into my face. She was close enough for me to receive the faint smell of her sweat. ''It's really a mother-son relationship. I always tell him he passed from his mother to me without even noticing the difference.''

I was to recall her remark subsequently.

''There you are,'' she concluded. ''I think you'll live now.''

''No septicemia?''

''No septicemia,'' she confirmed.

''The dogs are bored with blackberry picking,'' Ken announced, from which I inferred that he was, too.

''Well, we have enough for that summer pudding,'' I told him. ''Summer pudding?'' Richard echoed. ''What in hell is that?'' Ken threw me a familiar look. He had guessed what I was about to say — and didn't welcome it. He knew I was about to offer an invitation. And he has never encouraged me in dragging home everyone I ever meet — which I am rather prone to do, I admit. But the summer heat acted upon my ever-ready perversity in spite of his mute discouragement.

''How about coming to our place tomorrow and finding out? It won't be a heavy supper in this weather but Ken promised me a Vancouver summer pudding if I went blackberrying again. We call it ''Vancouver'' simply because we use Vancouver blackberries.''

It wasn't Ken's way to resolve our differences in public. Instead he looked carefully and at length at our two transparent bags. ''Davey's right,'' he said eventually. ''There's enough for a pudding and for freezing in a pie as well. How about a light supper, then? Eight o'clock? We can eat outside in this weather. And then Davey can entertain you as I shall have probably to go indoors and finish an article I keep putting off.''

Anna answered for both of them. Very quickly. ''You look as if you are very punctual.'' she said to him. ''Eight on the dot, right?''

Ken nodded. His face was expressionless and I felt a mild irritation in his refusal to look a little more encouraging. Then that and the threat of leaving me to play host was the price he was making me pay for his concurrence. His reproofs are never very exorbitant. . . .

In any event it was closer to eight-thirty the next evening when they arrived. So much for her ''on the dot'' routine, and my notions of Germanic punctuality. We had laid the red check tablecloth under the wisteria-festooned arbor, lit four candles, brought out the wine in its terra-cotta cooler, and switched on the garden lights just as the summer dusk was gathering.

Ken surveyed our handiwork as we awaited the click of the gate latch or the barking of the dogs — whichever came first. "Though I say it myself, it does all look quite attractive," he commented.

I remembered our Connecticut days. "In the east," I added, "we would have also lit the citronella candle, squirted *Raid* everywhere and rubbed *Off* on our bare arms and necks. Thank God for westcoast freedom from mosquitoes!"

Our shared complacency spilled like an invisible essence over the white metal garden chairs drawn up at the table on which Ken had placed a vase of sweet scented stock whose perfume filled the warm air.

From the road beyond the front of our house we heard a car pull up and its engine switch off. The dogs heard, too, and the canine din savaged the suburban quiet. Ken fled indoors to stir a pot while I hastened to the side gate lest our visitors be unduly scared by the racket from the dogs. I should perhaps have immediately suspected something by the noticeable change in demeanour in both of them since our shared blackberry picking. His boyish ebullience was withheld and no staccato torrent of works accompanied that faintly British accent when he greeted me. Indeed, he seemed petulant and it was Anna who had now become the chatterbox. Even before we were seated she had lavished praise on the garden setting, admired the now-quietened dogs, and twice informed us how fortunate they felt in being invited.

Ken and I exchanged looks. He kept on demurring at her unstinted encomiums by shaking his head and making lots of polite noises in his throat. After some fifteen minutes of all this her husband seemed to change his mind and came to life — vigorously.

"Dogs," he announced. "When they aren't shitting everywhere they've got their noses up each others asses before coming and licking you. They're filthy!"

Ken and I remained silent. Leif and Leila stayed at our feet: impervious. Anna, though, smiled sweetly at this sudden outburst. "Then you agree with me after all, Darling. They're no substitute for children. I think you are absolutely right! The maternal instinct shouldn't be sublimated by animals."

"That's not what I bloody well said, dammit! If dogs are plain anti-social, then having kids is grotesquely irresponsible with the Bomb around the corner."

Ken stood up. "I'll get some more white wine from the fridge." "If everyone talked like my husband," Anna remarked, looking at me as the only possible ally left, "there'd be no mankind to save from the nuclear war in a few years. I want a baby, you see, Davey. We can work out the nuclear problems afterwards." For one ludicrous moment I thought she might be actually making me a proposal but I was saved from idiotic comment by Richard errupting again.

"You wouldn't, you silly bitch, if you could imagine a fried infant or some lunatic monstrosity with cancerous lesions thrown in. Let's get *total* nuclear disarmament — and then we can talk about upping the birthrate. Do you know those bloody dogs can breed twice a year? If the Yanks get their way and use their bomb the world is soon going to be over-run with radio-active, mad dogs!"

A silence ensued. I made no effort to dispell it — guessing correctly that ultimately Anna would.

Out of the blue she asked what I thought of a recent play by Janice Ripley, an earnest local playwright. I started to say that I had mildly enjoyed it when Richard interrupted to say he thought it stupid, oldfashioned, and uncommitted to the basic issues of the times we were living through.

His opinions were one thing — bullying me with them quite another. "I gather you're not enthusiastic," I interjected, with as much sarcasm as I could muster. (Which is actually quite a lot). "It is certainly the most *direct* of her plays I've seen. No one could call it abstruse."

"No one in our circles would call *anything* abstruse," said Richard, with what I read as a nasty smile.

"My male chauvinist husband wouldn't like it anyway, because it's by a woman," Anna put in. "But I have to say I didn't care for it much either. It was too sentimental. But perhaps being European the play is just too North American for me."

"I think she's English-born and Jewish," I said, trying to simmer less with her.

"It's amazing, isn't it, how the Yanks can be so sloppily sentimental and yet so cynical with their aggressive imperialism and threats to destroy our planet." Richard stuck his thumb in the lapel of his jacket and leaned back on his chair across from me. I wondered if he was still irritated with me for using the word "abstruse".

I was saved further speculation by Ken's return. He had obviously heard much of our conversation crossing the lawn. "I think you're all making mountains out of vicious little molehills. Isn't the play about broken dreams and womanly dilemmas? I would've thought that still relevant in 1984 and that the dilemmas have a male equivalent, too."

Richard was eyeing his wife now. His look was not amiable. "Of course you could have told the thing was by a woman, even without a program. Only a woman could drip all that martyrdom. Or the penis-envy, come to that!"

"Anyone mind if I put on a Beethoven quartet?" I asked, suiting action to words and crossing to the outdoor stereo and searching for a cassette from the pile we had brought out before the advent of our guests.

"What, no Kenneth McKellar?" Richard asked, once more rocking back on his chair.

The business of putting on the E-Flat piano quartet saved me the onus of response. By the time I returned to the table the bickering between Richard and Anna had quickened and was to remain a constant throughout the rest of the evening. I must confess, however, that it impinged less and less upon me as they battled babies and bombs through Ken's home-made pâté, a shrimp omelette, and subsequent spinach salad — right up to the Summer Pudding: the ostensible reason for our assembly. As I listened to Richard's anti-American diatribe with increasing distaste I eyed his tautly handsome face and wondered if similar thoughts and attitudes had once coursed angrily through my brain — when my hair had been as devoid of grey as his and my skin as tightly smooth.

Such reflections were becoming depressingly familiar. More and more frequently I found myself slipping outside the confines of argument, escaping even a moral stance over things, to reflect instead on the *motivations* of those who championed this cause or that and to consider (albeit sadly) whether or not I had given up personal convictions to be, instead, a mere recorder and reflector of the passion and commitment of others. I had, on occasion, brought these musings to Ken's notice, but he had invariably dismissed them as foolish if not self-pitying.

This was a night when I was again tempted to repeat my misgivings to him. When they finally left, after two large post-dinner scotches (which I felt Richard could have well done without) we two sat there in the semi-darkness and made desultory conversation of a post-mortem nature over our departed guests.

"At least he really believes in his causes — however crudely he shouts them," I said. "I couldn't get that het up over anything."

But Ken was neither minded to defend Richard, nor let me off the hook. He tapped his fingers uncharacteristically on the tabletop. "That's nonsense, Kiddo. You can be as argumentative as the next when you want to be. Most of your friends would laugh their heads off if they heard you say that. As for him — nothing excuses the way he talks to her. Nothing! I don't *care* how committed he is to his bloody causes, that's no way to treat a friend, let alone a wife."

I stared towards Ken, even though I could scarcely make out his features since we had doused the guttering candles.

"He really did get to you, didn't he? I thought I was the only one thinking what an idiot he was making of himself — even if I did admire the fire he could stoke up."

There was a silence and I sensed that again I had brushed Ken the wrong way. I wasn't mistaken.

"That's half your trouble, Davey. Of course you thought you were the only one. Then at times like tonight you tend to act as if you *were* the only one out here."

I bridled at once. "Well, you hardly helped matters. You never once came to her rescue when he attacked her. If you ask me, you were sulking because they didn't make more fuss over your Vancouver summer pudding."

"I'm not talking about what I did or didn't do. That isn't the subject at the moment. Nor does the summer pudding come into it. I could see right away that neither of them much cared about what they ate. It's an instinct we cooks soon develop and which I suspect you know nothing about."

Being barely capable of boiling an egg, I was not going to contend with him in that quarter. "If you'd only speak up and say what you think while people are still around it wouldn't put me in such an egotistical light. As it is, I always appear the argumentative one and you the cool, objective type who disdains the cut and thrust of debate."

"We're not debating now, Davey. We're bickering! And that puts us on a par with the likes of the Cobhams."

I saw an escape from an incipient quarrel. "Well, Bonzo," (using my personal nickname for him) "I don't think I'm about to call you a bitch, tell you not to have children, and to drown the dogs."

When Ken laughed, even if it was short and strained, my spirits rose. Crisis averted. We rounded the evening out in the garden with a final scotch apiece and then took the dinnerware indoors, stacked the yard furniture and finally sauntered inside to bed.

As if an unspoken truce had been established, neither of us made more than scanty reference to either of them in the days that followed. Nor did we grumble when they failed to phone or in any way mark their appreciation of the Summer Pudding evening.

I think that both Ken and I felt that in some mysterious way the fractious couple had made negative impact upon us. It was only too easy, for instance, for me to see myself a little like a craven version of Richard, and I had the sense that Ken could as easily see himself sufficiently akin to Anna to be uncomfortable with the comparison. Fanciful perhaps. But that was it. Those oddball two made me feel strangely guilty and I could believe that Ken didn't like the idea of me thinking he was a bit like Anna in ducking from issues by embracing the prosaic.

But the whole matter was rendered rather academic when, some two weeks later, we were again walking the dogs and again in search for blackberries as ingredients for more Vancouver summer puddings. This time, though, the venue was in the southern heights of Jericho park; in the vicinity of Fourth Avenue where through bramble bushes, sappling willows and tall clumps of broom, could occasionally be seen glimpses of the Justice Institute above the slopes on the far side of the divided thoroughfare.

Not that either of us looked at or even spared a thought for that road and Jericho hill which bordered it to the south. Where we stood picking was a world very much its own. Quite free of other pickers we seemed alone with the cheerful sounds of redwing blackbirds and the occasional harsh chatter of a pair of pheasants we knew inhabited the dense scrubland surrounding us. The dogs also seemed to respond to this isolated tract above the marshes by staying close at hand and not persistently reminding us they preferred running to standing by bramble bushes which had such arcane attractions for their two masters.

At an earlier time in the year the nearby slopes were carpeted with blue lupin interspersed with white daisies. But in this August cocoon of heat there was only limp green as minor perforation to the tawny hillsides of hay, and the very first intimations of an approaching fall in the glow of crimson amid the yellowed leaves of the sumac. The air was still, the blackberries magnificently large in their unpicked plenty. We were contentedly self-absorbed as our Safeway plastic bags grew ever more swollen with their purple and our fingers ever more mauve in the stain of their juice.

Then, very faintly, as if from somewhere far from where we laboured, we heard singing. We exchanged glances, mystified — perhaps even resentful of the vocal trespassing. The dogs appeared to ignore the sound of distant massed voices, although it grew stronger every second. Instead they looked from one of us to the other, wagged their tails, and probably hoped we would at least move on from that one gigantic bush where we had lingered for nearly twenty minutes.

But we didn't. We just picked our berries more slowly. As the sound grew louder we could make out the tune and recognized some of the words. Our curiosity was piqued as we realized we were listening to the refrain from "We Shall Overcome".

"A labor demonstration?" I suggested.

"A Peace March, more likely," Ken offered — and, as it proved, more accurately. It seemed a long time before the procession was anywhere near us. Before that, we had already decided to edge a little closer to view the marchers. By now I had indeed abandoned berrying and with my bulging bag at my side, stood there awaiting them, my head stuffed with thoughts. This is no place to embark on a political essay but I can't help stating that my mind and emotions were once more in acute conflict. Then as now, I ached for the same goals as those strenuously singing "We Shall Overcome". I wanted The Bomb buried, the missiles abandoned, all nuclear weapons proscribed across the globe. I wanted, I prayed, for the peace of the world. Yet even as my heart stirred and I felt exhilarating solidarity with vulnerable mankind who simply wished to escape the thrall of the bellicose generals, I knew a bitter sense of Giant Manipulation at work. Oh yes, I could see so vividly the radio-active desert, the skinless dead, the living remnants of children. I would yield to none in the nightmare vision of man's inhumanity to man. After all, was it not my own generation who had revealed the moral stain of centuries in unveiling the stinking suppuration of the death camps and, within a matter of months, burned the lids from the eyes of myriads in Hiroshima and Nagasaki?

But try as I might, I could not shove my head in the morass of a nightmare Armageddon and leave my commonsense aside in the cause of salvation from a man-wrought Apocalypse. I could shudder at the prospect of an insupportable future but in the same breath I had to swell with ire at the preception of a cynical Marxist orchestration of fear and anger in the totalitarian cause of false-peace.

Of course there was the unthinkable horror of nuclear oblivion — but there was also the thinkable nadir of freedomless reality in those arid countries I had visited where friends sadly wrote off today in the faint promise of tomorrow. And I knew that the two were linked and I knew that *"better red than dead"* was the saddest twentieth century reflexion and the bottom line of moral bankruptcy. I was saved more bitterly paradoxical thought by Ken's bending down, clipping on Leif's leash, and calling out to me to move closer to him so that I, too, could see what my ears now told me was a vast concourse of people.

There they were, massed untidily across the four lanes of roadway, but protected by a police escort which both preceded and flanked them. I started to count but soon gave up. There were thousands — surely over fifty thousand, perhaps even one hundred thousand marching below the Justice Institute having earlier passed the Canadian Army barracks and with Jericho Hill School for the Deaf on the ridge peering down at them. . . .

Later the media seemed unanimous in stating that it was the largest demonstration of its kind in Vancouver's century of existence. It was stated proudly, too. My sense was that everyone was proud of the fact that our westcoast city evoked an infinitely more numerous response to anxiety over nuclear destruction than either Toronto or Montreal which were both roughly double the size.

But I run ahead of myself. Suddenly I hear a dog chain chink as Ken grabs my arm. "Look," he shouts, "look at the line just come into sight. The fourth and fifth persons nearest our side. See?"

I did. Immediately. In fact without his help I had already blotted out a multitude as two loomed for me as for him. There walk Anna and Richard. They are holding hands, swinging them in unison — which is how we can see they are joined. But it is their faces which nail our attention. Their expression — for the look is identical — is blissful. They are singing together, their lips thus also in unison. Both heads are held very high, their marching bodies taut with pride and youth. Just as they draw abreast of where we stand, invisible to them, they look at each other and I look straight into the eyes of Richard, dog-hater and lover of humanity. I have never read such happiness in a human face. They stop singing. They have to — for the look into each other is quickly followed by a kiss. Brief, because of the momentum of marching, but meaningful for all that. . . .

A further refrain was launched from the head of the column: Refuse the Cruise! It was straightway picked up by the waves of peace-walkers. I saw the lips of our Summer Pudding guests take up the defiant shout, but the joy never left their eyes. Then, with an abruptness that I found oddly shocking, it was all over. We found ourselves looking only at the napes of necks, unknown faces, or male and female flowing hair.